GO TELL IT
ON THE
MOUNTAIN™

Journey Along the 10 Trails of Wisdom

ROBERT WOLFF

Published by The Creative Syndicate

GO TELL IT ON THE MOUNTAIN™

Journey Along the 10 Trails of Wisdom

ROBERT WOLFF

Published by The Creative Syndicate
10400 Overland Road, Suite 143
Boise, Idaho, USA 83709

Copyediting by Lynette Smith
Book Interior Design by Betty Abrantes

Book Information: www.RobertWolff.com

Print edition ISBN: 978-1-937939-02-1
Electronic edition ISBN: 978-1-937939-03-8
First printing 2011
Library of Congress Control Number 2011961673

Introduction

They say everyone in life has a story and if we stop long enough to listen, we may just be inspired by what we hear.

Inspired enough to think a little differently.

Inspired enough to believe once again in ourselves and be awed by the synchronicity of Life and how the things in our lives seem to always work out for the best.

Inspired, perhaps, to become again like the kid we once were and allow ourselves to be open to the possibilities, instead of the problems, and to be led to the right people, in the right places, at the right times.

Such is the story of what you're about to read.

It's a story of what could happen to you and me, at any time, anywhere.

It's the story of how listening to our hearts, following our passion and never losing the love to learn, experience and explore, can change our lives and bring us the happiness we've always wanted, in ways we may have never imagined possible.

Robert

Contents

Chapter 1

| GRETCHEN'S STORY |

*M*y story could be that of any person.

I was a young woman living in New York City who came from a family that had all the pretenses of ideal, but in reality was far from it.

They say so much of who we are and what we become has its roots in our childhood.

Perhaps.

But as I grew older, I developed the conviction that I wouldn't become like my parents.

As a child, my dad was overly protective and unavailable. I knew he loved me, though he never found the right words or the time to tell me.

But it didn't matter.

At least inside my heart, I became the dad I needed.

Many a night as a young girl, I'd go to my darkened room and close my eyes and imagine my dad walking up the stairs to tuck me in for the night.

Oh, how I felt his hands brushing my hair as he pulled me close and hugged me tight as he whispered how much he loved his little princess.

Mom was always supportive, but she never really knew how to relate to me.

On the one hand, she was proud of me, of my ambitions and dreams, and she pushed me to achieve my goals.

On the other, she was jealous and resentful.

In her eyes, my whole life was in front of me, and yet her life clicked by faster and faster as each year passed.

My mom's life was spent doing the ultimate juggling act that never received much applause or great reviews: Raising a child, being a mom and a wife and carving out a career for herself.

Only now do I understand and am able to appreciate what she tried so hard to do.

Much of my life could be named after the television show called "In Search Of," for that's truly what it was, as I was in search of happiness and fulfillment in the faces of friends, family, relationships and, of course, career.

I never understood what was wrong with me, but I knew *something* was, because I could feel it gnawing inside.

Constantly.

But why? I kept asking myself.

After all, I was following what friends and family and society were telling me I needed.

And every time I listened to them, I felt empty.

Very soon, I came to believe I would never be filled.

I worked hard in school and made good grades.

I interviewed with the top companies and received offers from most.

I landed a cushy job with one of the most desired companies and was filling my portfolio with more money and experience than I could've asked for.

My job took me to exciting destinations around the world, filled with glamorous people who were enjoying "the good life," just like me.

Some act.

With each new job, I was advancing in status but failing in life.

And through it all, there was no one I could tell how I felt, much less anyone who'd truly *understand*.

I sought answers through relationships, but quickly concluded that Mr. Right had turned into Mr. Right Now; and he, too, had problems he didn't understand or wasn't willing to deal with.

We were two people who needed to be fixed, and neither of us had the tools or know-how to do it.

It was about that time in my life that I met Chloe, a sweet older woman I'd talk with every now and then on the way to work or on weekends at the coffee shop on the corner of 7th and Lexington.

Chloe was the epitome of elegance and simplicity. Her statuesque frame, high cheekbones, blond hair and blue eyes caused more than one man to stare.

Whenever we spoke, the conversation was always about me, my job, my family, what movies I'd seen or new places where I'd eaten.

It was me… me… me.

Then she disappeared.

Many weeks went by and I didn't see Chloe.

When I asked around, no one knew where she was, much less where she lived. I could only hope that she was okay.

One day as I walked into the coffee shop, there she was.

My heart filled with relief and joy. For some reason, this woman and I had clicked, and I just felt so good inside whenever I was with her.

I asked where she had been all those weeks.

"Do you *really* want to know?"

"Of course!"

It was then that she began to describe her journey.

A journey to a place she called *"the Mountain."*

As she began to describe her experience, every fiber of my being became locked into her eyes and words.

She was saying things I wanted to hear.

She was saying things I needed to hear.

She was saying things I had to hear.

She was saying things I had never heard.

Never had I met anyone who spoke with such peace, such assurance, such believability and such inner strength as this woman.

Then I realized something.

For the first time in my life, I had finally met the one person who had "figured it out."

Like a lost traveler for days who walked the hot and parched desert sands, I finally found the oasis of water for a soul that begged to be nourished.

My soul.

Three days later, I boarded American Airlines flight 724, bound for South America.

And so it began.

My journey to the Mountain...

Chapter 2

THE JOURNEY TO SOUTH AMERICA

*T*he flight from New York takes just under five hours.

My plane touches down at 5 p.m., and once I make it through customs—thanks in no small part to my pocket English-to-Spanish translator—I find the carousel with my luggage spinning around.

I have 45 minutes to catch the one-flight-a-day puddle-jumper to the town of Partangia. If I miss it, I'm up the proverbial creek without a paddle.

I quickly grab my bags and look all over for the sign for "Avianca."

Lost in the maze, there it is; "Avianca Upstairs," the arrow points.

I lug my suitcases up what seems like steps from the Empire State Building. Out of breath, I reach the ticket window, but in front of me are two lines of at least 75 people—as in 75 people in each line.

As I watch the second hand sweep the clock, my heart races with nervousness while my body telegraphs stress to those around me.

Three women who look college age are behind me watching my frenetic back-and-forth pacing. One of the girls who speak English asks where I am going. I tell her "To the town of Partangia," and she politely reminds me that the flight is leaving in 35 minutes.

As if I didn't know.

She then turns to her friends and speaks in Spanish twice as fast as my Rosetta Stone Spanish DVDs played.

So much for being fluent in 30 days.

The three of them look at me and smile, as if I was the amigo of today's joke, then two of them leave their place in line and begin talking to people ahead of me, while the third walks quickly to the front and begins speaking to the ticket agent.

What the heck is going on here?

A few seconds later, I hear a loud whistle and look in front of me.

As everyone stares, I see the ticket agent and the college girl quickly motioning me to come forward.

As I make it to the front of the line saying, "Excuse me" and "Thank you" in the nicest Spanish sounding English I know, the college girl tells me she explained my dilemma to the agent and she will help me now.

I thank her and her friends and turn to everyone now standing behind me, and wave and tell them "Muchas Gracias" in my new native Spanish tongue.

Thank God I don't have to speak loud English, since they look like they understand.

The agent quickly makes short order of my seeming impossible situation and summons a young baggage handler over and tells him to help me.

With no time to check my luggage, the young man grabs both handles and heaves them off the ground—why do I always pack too much?—and leads the way.

We make it to the security baggage scan and the young man tells the guard my situation. The guard looks at both bags and motions like he wants me to open them so he can physically inspect the contents.

Oh great… now's the time to start earning your pay.

The flight leaves in 25 minutes and we're 10 minutes from the gate.

Trying to stay composed with all the sweetness I can muster and with a big cheesy smile I picked up from years of watching the Miss America contest, the guard looks at me as he listens to the baggage man.

He pauses for a few seconds, then with grumbles and much hesitation, motions me through.

As I walk briskly past him, I give him one big "Muchas Gracias, Señor," as he quickly turns his head and looks away and motions to the next passenger to head his way.

I made it, but there is still forever to go.

I never knew two legs could walk so fast.

Thank goodness for treadmills and stair steppers, because by the time my two legs arrive at the gate, they are quivering like a wet dog standing outside in the cold.

Oh, and my baggage-handling friend?

He must've been part draft horse and part greyhound.

How such a wiry, spindly young guy could carry two heavy suitcases so far, so fast, is beyond me and well worth the extra pesos that make his face light up.

I have 10 minutes to doors closed.

My bags are hand-checked and carried out on the tarmac to be loaded on the plane.

As I work my way to the noisy back of the crowded stuffy plane, I don't even notice all the stares.

I'm only thinking one thing…

If this is the beginning of my adventure, what on earth have I gotten myself into?

Chapter 3

THE ARRIVAL AT PARTANGIA

So far, the flight has lasted 2 hours, and it is the longest 120 minutes I can remember.

Now I know what a sardine feels like.

But I shouldn't complain.

For two hundred dollars, you too can get on board and enjoy all the legroom a 9-year old would ever need, and they'll even throw in, for free, an hour and a half of turbulence that'll make you toss your cookies.

The things we put ourselves through.

As we circle in the darkness near our destination, I keep looking out the window, wondering if we were ready to do the vertical.

Were we running low on fuel?

Suddenly, the lights go on, on the ground below the plane.

We are circling the airport and somebody has to turn on the runway lights just so we can land!

A few minutes later, as the wheels touch earth, my tush, hands and face slowly began to pry themselves loose from the vise-grip they've been in.

As we taxi, I think I've already said 50 "Thank you God's," and the plane hasn't even stopped yet.

Finally it does.

A few minutes pass and as the flight attendant opens the door, almost immediately the cabin fills with a balmy warm, tropical breeze.

This is definitely not New York City.

I grab my carry-on and head towards the door and walk down the steps to the tarmac.

I look in front of me and there, standing at the only doorway entrance to the airport, are two soldiers armed with machine guns, and both men's eyes are glued to me like I'm a terrorist.

I calmly walk past them.

To my immediate left is the only baggage carousel in the airport.

There, through a small hole in the wall, I'm guessing our bags will be pushed through and will land on the carousel.

I stand near it and try not to call any attention to myself as I look all around me.

A few minutes go by and the carousel begins to move.

As my two bags come through, I grab each and head to the customs desk.

It is the only one, too.

I hand my passport to the customs agent

He takes his sweet time as he slowly pages through my passport, looking at all the places my "exciting life" has taken me.

Right now, so many things are racing through my mind.

Will this guy think I have money, since it looks like I travel so much?

Will he call some friends or send me to a cab driver who is going to take me somewhere no one will find me and take my money or, perhaps, worse?

The longer his geography lesson lasts, the more anxious I feel.

A few more seconds pass and he reaches for his stamp and stamps my passport and hands it back to me.

I am free to go.

With bags in tow, I make my way outside to the taxi stand.

There, lined up near the curb, are what have to be at least 20 taxis.

Great; I'll quickly grab the first one and be on my way.

Wrong.

You would think these guys are having a convention the way they are huddling together smoking cigarette after cigarette, chit-chatting, no doubt, about how much money they *aren't* making and the dumb gringo across the street who's just waiting for one of them to open his trunk.

One brave soul does.

Without a word, he grabs one of my bags and it stuffs the tiny trunk, which now becomes completely full.

The other bag will be my escort sitting in the back seat next to me as it rubs the door and my shoulder.

I get in.

We take off.

His radio is playing mariachi as I look around and admire the photos of his family plastered on the dashboard, while the rosary hanging from the rear view mirror keeps perfect time with the music and the potholes in the street.

His voice comes back to me just loud enough over the radio for me to hear...

"Where are you going?" is what I guess he's saying.

I yell back, "To Javiar's Shop on Revolution Street!"

Javiar, Chloe told me, is the man I should ask for once I arrive in town. He will know how to get me to the Mountain.

Right now, my only hope is that my chauffeur will know whoI'm talking about.

He does.

Forty minutes later, the car eases its way down a long unmarked street with street lamps that are either burned out or flickering.

The car stops.

The driver motions and points to his right to what looks like a small unmarked garage with a roll-down door with a large padlock attached.

"Javiar's, *sí*," comes from the cabby's lips, as he points to the shop.

"This is Javiar's shop?"

"*Sí.*"

Oh great.

The place is closed and not a breath of life from anyone, and nothing is moving on the empty street.

I'm beat, and I've got to find a place to crash.

A few moments pass.

Somehow the cabby realizes the situation and sees my frustration as he looks back at me in his rearview mirror as I'm looking for the word "hotel" in my pocket translator.

Before I can find it, he takes off.

Ten minutes later, we pull up to the steps of the hotel and probably the only one in town.

As the driver begins to unload my suitcases, I take out a wad of pesos and place them in his hand and thank him.

As he opens his hand and counts what's inside, his face lights up with a huge smile.

He reaches for my hand and excitedly shakes it up and down repeatedly.

With a big smile still on face, he hops in his cab, looks back, honks his horn and waves his hand out the window as he speeds off.

The hotel man who comes out to greet me is watching from a distance, and as he grabs my bags, I ask him, "Are all cab drivers as happy as him?"

"How many pesos did you give him?"

"I don't know, probably a thousand; why?"

"You'd be happy too. That's a month's salary."

After being up nearly 20 hours, I'm getting my second wind and amazingly, I don't want this day to end.

Yet, I know tomorrow will be a new day; and for the first time in a long time, I'm excited to see what it's about to bring.

.

Chapter 4

THE NEXT DAY—THE MEETING WITH JAVIAR

*H*aving just had one of the most restful nights of sleep I've enjoyed in years, I awake to sounds of birds singing and *not* horns honking.

So much for the excitement of "The Big City."

After a hot shower, I grab a pair of jeans and a white T-shirt and sandals and head downstairs for breakfast.

The food is extraordinary.

Fresh eggs, warm baked bread, fresh fruit pastries with powdered white sugar—yeah, what diet?—and juice so fresh you would think they picked it that morning.

They probably did.

After breakfast, I ask the woman behind the reception desk how far Javiar's shop is.

"Ten minute cab ride or a 20-minute walk."

Off go the sandals and on go the Reeboks.

With the crude little map the receptionist drew, I hold it out of in front of me as I hit the sidewalk and start walking.

Amazingly, I navigate my way with no problem to Revolution Street and to the front of Javiar's Shop.

I quickly fold the piece of paper and tuck it into my back pocket and step inside.

There, behind an old wooden table, is a tall, tanned, bespectacled man who looks in his 60s, with a beautiful full head of silver-gray hair.

He looks up and smiles.

"Are you Javiar?"

"Yes. May I help you?"

I walk and look around his store.

"Gee, I sure hope so."

"Would you like to buy one of my wood or stone carvings?"

Seconds go by.

"I was told to see you as soon as I arrived in town."

"Where are you from?"

"New York City."

"A long way from home, aren't you?"

"Yes."

"Tell me, who told you to see me?"

"A woman… no… actually, a *friend*. A friend named Chloe."

"This Chloe, can you describe her?"

"Well, she's probably mid-50s, tall, blond hair, blue eyes, big cheek bones, strikingly beautiful and—"

"Quiet and somewhat shy?"

He catches me by surprise.

"Why… why, yes!"

Javiar is smiling.

"Of course. Please… sit down here in front of my table, and shall we talk?"

"Yes, I'd like that."

We both sit down.

"How is it that I may help you Señorita?"

"I want to go to the Mountain."

"Señorita, there are many mountains in our beautiful country and—"

"—No, no, no. I want to go to *the Mountain* to meet Simole."

He pauses.

"Oh… Simole. Are you sure?"

I'm getting flustered.

"Yes! Javiar, I've traveled over 2,000 miles and have waited all my life for this moment, and I want to meet Simole! Now can you take me to him?"

Javiar leans back in his chair and folds his arms.

"No, I'm sorry. I can't you to him. But... I can take you to her."

"Oh... her. I didn't know he was a she. Do you really know her and who I'm talking about?"

"Don't worry, Señorita, you've come to right place."

A few customers come into his shop and glance back at me repeatedly as they engage Javiar in conversation while he tries to do a little business.

I get up and walk over to the soda machine and put in a few pesos to get a Coke.

After my least peso drops in the machine, out pops the smallest bottle of Coke I've ever seen. I grab it, pop the cap on the outside of the machine and head outside.

I pull up one of the rickety old wooden chairs in front of his store and watch as the dilapidated buses crammed with riders, cars bellowing smoke, bicycles, motorcycles, trucks and people go by.

A few minutes later, Javiar calls my name—"Señorita"—as he waves for me to come back inside.

I get up, taking a last swig from the bottle, and head inside.

With a testing look and after giving me some time to think about things, Javiar begins to speak. "So, you still want to see Simole?"

"Yes, of course."

"Then please sit down."

I grab a chair.

He begins...

"So be it."

"The journey will take at least a day, maybe two, by foot and horseback and over the most difficult terrain you can imagine.

"There will be times when you will wish you never would have met me and will probably want to shoot me."

He sees the uneasy expression on my face.

"But, there will be times when your breath will be taken away by all the beauty and splendor of the sights your eyes will see.

"The journey will be long and difficult, but if you make it—and I think you have the cajangas to do it—then you will be blessed in ways I, nor your friend Chloe, nor anyone else could ever tell you.

"Do you still want to go?"

"Yes!"

"Then be here tomorrow morning at 8 a.m. and take only a few clothes and a change of shoes."

"Do I need to do anything else?"

"Yes, I'd like you to do me a favor."

"Sure."

He hands me a pen and a sheet of paper.

"I'd like you to sign your name on this piece of paper."

Thinking he is a collector of names and signatures of people he has met, I gladly oblige.

As I hand Javiar the signed piece of paper, he smiles as he lays the paper inside an old wooden box on his desk and puts the lid back on it.

I thank him for his help and leave his shop until I see him again.

Twenty-two hours later.

Chapter 5

DAY TWO: 8 A.M.—THE TRIP TO THE JUNGLE

I never realized how hard it would be to pack for the trip. Javiar told me to bring only a few clothes and a change of shoes, so maybe he won't care if I bring just a few extra things.

I arrive at Javiar's shop at a few minutes before eight.

Looks like I beat him there; the door is still locked.

A few minutes go by and the garage door rolls up, and inside are Javiar and one other man.

As he reaches outside of the gate to unlock the padlock, Javiar bellows, "Buenos Dias, Señorita," and motions for me to come in.

We exchange greetings as he looks down with a big grin at the suitcase I bring in.

"Going on a vacation?"

I smile, not knowing if he's joking or saying "Dump the Samsonite, Sista" in a nice way.

"Why… why yes, I am, thank you."

He leaves the shop and goes to the room in back and comes out holding a big burlap coffee bag and throws it to me to catch.

"For where you're going, this is the only suitcase you'll need."

Embarrassed that I probably look like such a dufus and not wanting him to see all the clothes I "snuck" in, I take the suitcase and burlap bag to an area out of sight of his shop and quickly exchange contents.

I hurry back.

"There, all done. Are we ready?"

He admires the coffee sack half-filled with clothes.

16

"I see you've taken my advice and are traveling light."

He points to his friend.

"This is Fernando, and he will be your guide."

We shake hands.

"Fernando is a most trusted friend and knows the journey better than anyone, so you can trust him Señorita."

"Great. Are we ready to go?"

Javiar looks over at Fernando.

"Not quite yet.

"For Fernando to make the journey he will have to leave his job and family, and we wouldn't want him to do that without a few pesos in his pocket, now, would we?"

"Well, no, of course not. How much should I give him?"

"Let's see… I think 500 pesos would be fine."

I dig through my pocket book in my hip sack. "Sure, no problem." I hand the money to Fernando, who tells me "Muchas Gracias" with a smile.

With money in hand, Fernando speaks a few last words in Spanish to Javiar as they both chuckle out loud, shakes his hand and then quickly motions me to follow him.

I bid goodbye to Javiar as he follows Fernando and me out of his shop.

As we're walking up the street, I hear Javiar behind us.

"Please come back after you have returned from your journey."

I look back and wave. "I will. I will."

Fernando takes my bag and throws it in the back of his rickety old beat-up Chevy pickup truck.

Trying my best to figure out how to open the passenger door, he motions to me that I can't open it from the outside and he has to do it from the inside.

As I get in the truck and sit down, I feel the coil springs sticking up through the seat cushion and poking me through the thick woven blanket he's laid over the seat. Inside, the truck is covered with more dirt and dust than an old Hoover vacuum bag.

The truck finally cranks over and starts.

I look out my side mirror, which is hanging by two pieces of hay baling wire around the steel tubular frames where it used to be mounted.

As the truck sputters and coughs smoke as we move forward, I look in the mirror and see Javiar waving.

If only I could know what he's thinking.

Chapter 6

THE JOURNEY TO AND ARRIVAL AT THE MOUNTAIN—A MOST UNLIKELY OF WELCOMES AND WHERE A LIFE IS ABOUT TO BE CHANGED

The journey to the Mountain took us a day and a night, over the most beautiful and brutal terrain I have ever experienced.

And like a genius, I just had to time my visit during the hot summer season.

The smoldering heat and humidity and afternoon downpours were only the beginning.

Fernando must've chosen the boniest swayback horse he could find for me to ride.

My horse followed behind Fernando, who kept singing the same Spanish ballads over and over as we made our way up and down the rocky trails. With every step the animal took, it seemed, I was asking myself: What the heck kind of crazy hair-brained whim was I following?

One sleepless mosquito-bitten night was enough for me, and with the new day breaking and sun shining I'm beginning to wonder if I should just turn back now and forget about this crazy adventure.

It's too late.

Fernando has our horses ready and is holding the reins, waiting for me to climb up on the saddle and take them.

With a forced smile and "Gracias, Fernando," I do, and we begin the new day towards the Mountain.

A couple of hours pass.

As we reach what looks to be a field, Fernando stops singing.

He looks back at me with a smile as he points his fingers forward.

I straighten up and look more awake as we move closer.

As my horse slowly makes its way to a grassy clearing at the bottom of the Mountain, an older man begins walking towards us.

I don't know this man, yet Fernando doesn't seem surprised by his appearance.

As we approach, the man begins to speak. "Welcome, Friend. Welcome! May I ask your name?"

"Gretchen."

"Well, Gretchen, my name is Maxwell, and it's good to have you here.

"Come and relax." He takes my hand and helps me off the horse as Fernando takes my horse's reins and walks off to a stream, where the two animals can be watered and rested.

"Please, sit down." He motions for me to sit next to him on the fallen tree.

"Here's a cool glass of water." My eyes lock onto his as I listen.

"Sit back. I know why you're here."

"You do?"

"Yes, of course."

A few moments pass.

"Gretchen, may I tell you a story?"

I begin to relax.

"Yes. Please."

His story begins…

"Gretchen, many years ago when I wore a younger man's clothes, my life was much different than it is this day.

"As a young boy, I grew up in a family with one older brother, and it was then, inside my young impressionable mind, that I began sowing the seeds of how unfair life was.

"You could say that growing up inside the four walls of our home was demanding and difficult at best.

"My father was a good man, but a strong and stern disciplinarian who found it difficult to accept who he was and even more difficult to say the words, 'I love you.'

"Even to his wife.

"Dad always seemed unavailable.

"'Not now, I've got work to do,' he would quickly tell me whenever I asked if we could play catch with the baseball.

"And after work was done? Well, he would tell me, 'It's too late' and 'We'll do it another time.'

"But that time never came.

"Perhaps, through the pangs of guilt, he tried making up for his unavailability by opening his wallet.

"But his wallet couldn't contain enough money to take the place of just one 'I'm really proud of you, Kid.'

"As a young child, I grew up believing my brother was put on this earth as a punishment for something I did.

"He was older, stronger, faster and smarter, and Dad didn't hide his feelings that my brother was his favorite son. 'A real man after my own heart,' he would say, 'and, by golly, cut from the same cloth.'

"If only Dad's eyes would've opened wider, he would've seen his other 'little man' standing beside him, draped in that same cloth."

Maxwell pauses and looks around.

"Mom was the most wonderful woman. A sweet woman, quiet in her demeanor and with a backbone and not a wishbone.

"Mom gave us love that a thousand dads could never duplicate.

"Hers was a love without conditions.

"Hers was a love that only *mothers* in deeds—and not just with title of 'Mother'—can give.

"But, for me, even that wasn't enough.

"As I grew older, deep inside I made a vow to myself that only strengthened with each birthday that passed: I would never be like my dad.

"But I was wrong."

He looks at me with guilt written on his face.

I smile back with reassurance that it's okay.

"Once I received my high school diploma, I immediately found work. Forget college; who needed it? Work was my savior, and every day I would return to its hallowed hallways and worship it, just as faithful as any devout believer.

"In a very short time, I was making more money than Dad could ever dream of and was holding the ticket onboard the success train bound for Happyville.

"Then I met Elizabeth.

"If ever there was a woman who must've made the Almighty smile with joy at the marvel of Its creation, it was her.

"Elizabeth came from good stock; her father and mother and their families came from wealth and privilege.

"But Elizabeth was different.

"She may have grown up with a silver spoon, but for reasons unknown to her family and friends, she worked hard to replace it with the utensils of a life lived by simple, common folks who valued people more than portfolio.

"It wasn't long after we met that we were married; and in less than a year, Elizabeth was carrying our baby.

"Oh my goodness, those were happy times.

"Not knowing what new experience each day would bring.

"Not having all the answers and not giving a damn if we did.

"We were figuring out this thing called Life along the way and enjoying every minute of it.

"Then Christina was born and suddenly our world changed.

"Or perhaps I should say *my world* changed.

"Even though I had always wanted and now had a family that any man would've been proud of, they became my foster family.

"For too long, I had stopped working like a crazy man to spend time with Elizabeth and the new baby.

"I had neglected work—and make no mistake, work can be a jealous mistress.

"Without thinking much about it, I began staying at the office just a few minutes later each day. Those minutes turned to hours, and the days turned to weeks and years.

"Forget family.

"My work was my life, and it was the only thing I knew that truly mattered. After all, I kept telling myself, I was doing it for my family, and of course they would understand."

As I listen, my life flashes before my eyes. Maxwell could be describing me.

He continues. "My ascent was dramatic. I was now CEO. Equally dramatic was my earning power; whatever I wanted I could buy.

"Except one.

"My family back.

"By then, it was too late. One day I came home and the house was empty. Elizabeth had taken Christina and left.

"Then, it dawned on me. For years, the house had always been empty. Ours was only a house; never a home.

"Elizabeth and Christina felt it.

"Now I felt it.

"It was there, on the fateful day, that I felt shock waves like I had never known. *I had become my father*."

He pauses.

I sit in stunned silence as I keep wondering why this stranger is telling me such personal details of his life and his pain.

Maxwell senses my confusion and nods his head to reassure me all will be well.

"Gretchen, life can be very forgiving and gives us many chances to get it right when we mess things up, and I was hoping Elizabeth would do the same.

"And so we agreed that we would try one more time.

"A fresh new start. A chance to rekindle the embers that needed to be stirred again to start the fire that would now be the warmth for our home.

"But it was never to be.

"That night, on the way back from her parent's estate, Elizabeth and Christina's lives ended at the hands of a driver who hit them head on."

"Oh my God!" I gasp.

My eyes fill with tears as I sit quietly listening to this man I never met, as his words stung like wasps on the honeycomb of my soul.

Once again, my life flashes back before my eyes.

I may never have known the loss of two loved ones so close, but I knew all too well about emptiness. For all my life, I had come to believe that the emptiness I felt was something no one or nothing could fill.

And for the first time in my life, I am at a loss for words.

Maxwell pauses and looks around for a few seconds and then begins to speak.

"Doctors say it was instantaneous and they didn't suffer any pain. But even after all these years, why can't I tell my heart the same?"

Tears are flowing as I wipe my eyes. I try to finding the right words to say, but I can't.

"Life passes so quickly," he says. "We think we have forever and there'll always be tomorrow, but someday there won't.

"I found out much too late just what I had and what I lost, and to this day the words of Tennyson keep echoing in my head: 'It is better to have love and lost, than never to have loved at all.' Oh, but what would I give to love them just once more.

"My life changed after the loss of Elizabeth and Christina.

"And yes, some things were still the same. I was still CEO, heading a company with record profits and given stock options and bonuses that now carried eight digits on my bank balances, but none of it mattered anymore. Not one damn bit of it.

"What price can one put on happiness? Not superficial materiality. What would the richest and most successful people in their graves give just to fill their lungs with one more breath of this gift called Life?

"I'll tell you…*everything*."

I'm silent as my life story is racing full speed like a movie playing inside my head.

"Oh, Maxwell, you are so right!

"I have the great job, the great apartment, closets overflowing with more clothes and shoes than I need and bank accounts filled with enough money that I could have stopped working years ago, but it never feels like enough. It's never felt like enough."

Maxwell begins once again…

"It was about this time that a friend of Elizabeth told me of an incredible experience she had.

"All the experiences in her life brought her to a place that called for more answers than she was getting from friends, family, relationships, or career.

"Her soul hungered for the manna society couldn't give her, and she found it where I did." He extends his arms in front of him. "Here. Here… at this place where *you* will find it too."

I pause and look at everything surrounding me. "Here?"

"Here, Gretchen. Here, on the Mountain."

Maxwell leans forward and smiles. "My journey to the Mountain began many years ago and it has never ended. For I don't think it ever will.

"Each time I journey along its trails, I always learn something new, something I never realized or quite understood before.

"And I know it'll be the same for you."

I keep looking around at the mountains and jungle surrounding me.

"Gretchen, I don't know your story, nor do I think I need to.

"Is it possible to explain all the events of your life to one person and have them truly understand you in ways you want and need to be understood?"

"I don't think so."

"I don't either. "Yes, Gretchen, all that matters is that you're here. All that matters is that you've listened to the voice inside of you that's been calling you all these years."

I smile.

"I am, Maxwell. I am."

"Gretchen, you've taken the steps that most people want to but never will, because of fear, ridicule and uncertainty.

"It's been a long tough road, but you've made it. You've made it to the Mountain.

"And what you're about to learn is going to change your life forever."

Chapter 7

THE MEETING OF SIMOLE

As I get up from the hollowed out tree stump where I have been comfortably listening—anything is better than sitting on the back of a bony, swayback horse—I see an older woman and a group of nine other people walking towards me.

Before I can let fully sink in the story I just heard, Maxwell pats me on the shoulder and says with a reassuring smile, "Gretchen, *this* is Simole."

My heart starts beating faster as my eyes lock into hers.

She smiles and reaches out and takes hold of my hands.

This is the woman that changed Chloe and Maxwell's life.

Simole is radiant.

Her hair is long and flowing, silvery gray with beautiful strands of black.

Her warm, deep brown eyes set in the round moon face atop her 5'4" frame.

Her brown olive skin caressed by a life in sunshine and fresh air.

She gives me a smile that melts my heart. Her soft hands hold and protect mine as I hear her voice that soothes my soul.

I haven't found Simole. I've found the grandmother I never had.

"My dear, welcome. What is your name?"

"Gretchen. My name is Gretchen."

"Well, Gretchen, my name is Simole, and it's so good to have you here."

"Oh, thank you, Simole. It feels so good to be here."

"Come. Let us show you where you'll stay."

So it begins.

My journey to the Mountain with Simole and her people.

As we wind our way through the manicured path, not a word is spoken.

We stop in a small open clearing surrounded by trees, and Simole points to the right.

"Over there. That is where you'll stay."

I look and see a thatched-roof hut made of bamboo.

It isn't the Ritz, but I'm not complaining.

Simole smiles.

"Relax Gretchen, you've had a long journey. Frederica will show you where you may find water and bathe. I'll be back this evening, and then we will talk."

And with those words, Simole walks off with the eight others.

The questions are racing through my mind right now.

Who are those people?

Where are they going?

Where does Simole live?

Frederica, a young woman who I'm guessing is about my age, is tall, thin and gorgeous, and she gestures for me to follow her.

As we walk about 100 steps behind the hut, there, at the bottom of a ravine, is a pool of water fed by a small waterfall.

"Here is where you may bathe and gather water to drink."

As we make it back to the hut, I open the woven bamboo door and look inside.

Let's see... great room, plenty of space, park view; easily ten G's a month in the Upper West Side.

Placed on a small table near the window is a bowl filled with the most vibrantly colored fruit I've seen.

I stare, hoping it isn't for decoration.

Frederica chuckles.

"Yes, please eat. It's for you."

I don't need to be told twice.

Chapter 8

THE FIRST EVENING AND MY TALK WITH SIMOLE

*A*s the moon mists its light through the trees, I'm sitting on the porch of the hut in some sort of trance, watching my life change before my eyes like a spectator watches a sports game.

I don't notice Simole's arrival until her words snap me out of my trance.

"Thinking of things deep?"

"Oh, I'm sorry. I was just trying to let it all soak in."

"My dear, there is nothing to be sorry about. You have come a lot further than you think."

"You really think so?"

"Close your eyes, Gretchen. I want you to think for a moment of the person you were the day you left for Partangia and tell me who that person was."

I pause, as it takes me a while to switch gears and think of the words.

"Well… I was anxious… uptight… mad… cocky… unsure… determined… scared… and—"

"Good. Now think of the person you were the day you arrived in town."

It's getting easier.

"I am still anxious and determined, but I feel like I have finally achieved something that means something, and the excitement of the unknown makes me feel energized and alive!"

"Yes. You were coming out of your cocoon, weren't you?"

"I never thought of it that way, but yes, it felt like a whole other part of me was finally given the okay to come out and see what I've been missing."

"And tell me, how do you feel right now?"

"You know, Simole, I've never met you before. I don't know who those people were who were with you, and I don't know what, if anything, I'm going to discover here, but I don't care. I can honestly say I really don't care, because already I feel like I've grown more and learned more about myself in these few days than I have in 30 years, and that feels pretty good."

She takes hold of my hands.

"Oh, Gretchen, we are going to enjoy our time together. This I can promise you."

I look into her eyes and every part of me says she is right.

"Tomorrow we shall have breakfast, so get a good night's rest."

And with that, Simole walks out of sight.

Tomorrow can't arrive fast enough.

Chapter 9

THE NEXT MORNING—THE DAY I BEGIN MY JOURNEY ON THE MOUNTAIN

"Miss Gretchen… Miss Gretchen," calls a voice outside my window.

I mumble, as my mouth stays buried in the pillow.

"Uh-huh."

"Soon it will be time for breakfast."

I struggle to coax my mind into making my body move.

"Okay. Be right there."

After a quick bath and shower courtesy of mother Nature, 100 steps away, I slip into a pair of Calvins (shorts and loose, of course), a pullover and hiking boots and look around for which way to go.

I hear my name being called.

"Gretchen."

I look around.

Frederica motions me to follow her. "This way."

We walk along a path about 100 yards from my hut and there, under the shade of magnificent jungle trees, is Simole's home.

The home, or I should say compound, is perfectly blended into its surroundings. It's a single-level curved structure with roof and sides covered in vines budding beautiful flowers that wrap around trees and with trees in the middle of the home. It's breathtaking—as if the jungle had constructed it itself.

As I admire the home and surroundings, I'm told we will be having breakfast in the garden.

We make our way around to the back of the home. I see Simole and her friends waving to me.

Simole greets me with a smile and a hug. "Hope you're hungry."

"Yes, I am."

Moments later, a young man and woman begin bringing out a feast that would have made the Romans jealous.

Scrambled eggs, platters of exotic fruit, a big bowl filled with a mixture of whole grains, vases of goat milk and fresh mineral water.

I must have died and gone to heaven.

As I begin reaching for the fruit, Simole and the rest of those sitting around the table look down.

"Let's us close our eyes and be thankful for the blessings of the Universe, the bounty for our bodies, the food for our souls and our new friend Gretchen."

"Thank you," I say under my breath, looking over with a smile at Simole.

After a few minutes of our indulging in such a delicious feast, Simole looks at me and speaks. "Gretchen, you've come a long way to be here. The journey has been difficult, has it not?"

"Yes."

"My dear, you have embarked on the journey within. A search for understanding. About ourselves. The world. And our need to know why. Something deep inside you has led you to this path, to me, and to the Mountain.

"This will be your *new* start. The start of a new life. And a path, *your path,* that will lead you to *The Answer.*

"For it is there you will meet the wisest person you will ever know and hear what the wisest of all persons will reveal to you.

"In my 60 years of life on this earth, I have known many who wish for answers, yet few who truly *want* them.

"You, Gretchen, are among the few."

I smile.

"To find the answers, many have wanted to give up, and perhaps you were one of them. Yet something inside of you said, '*No, not this time.*'

"For I ask you, is it not what you wish to leave behind and what your soul has called you to find, that has pushed you to take every step along the unknown dangerous path to this mountain to find the answers your heart has hungered for?"

I nod.

"And I ask you Gretchen, is there not something deep within your heart, telling you that unless you listen to the Universe and the Great Creator calling you from within, to find your own spirit path, your life will continue to be a life of years wasted and promises unfulfilled?"

I pause.

"Yes."

Breakfast… I stopped eating long ago.

Simole reclines back in her chair and smiles at her family and then at me. "Each journey begins the same: a soul that searches for truth and to find The Way.

"You see Gretchen, for too many precious years of their adult lives, many people have worshipped at the altar of the world's opinion, read from the 'good book' of success and drunk from the chalice of indifference.

"And every day, the feelings of emptiness will not go away."

I nod my head and whisper under my breath, "Yes."

"The marriage failed or teetering near.

"The bigger house that only feels cold and empty.

"The career never fulfilling.

"Possessions that own them, their time, money and happiness.

"Friends and family who never really understand them.

"A moral compass of bearings lost.

"And time, that only passes more quickly with each new day.

"And this, say some, is the *gift* of life?

"Some gift."

Simole is speaking words that are cutting right to my heart.

"Yet all is never lost. For is not each day a new day, a chance to start anew?

"For does not Life wipe yesterday's slate clean with each new dawn?

"And does the Sun not shine equally on, or the seconds tick the same for, one who is happy or sad, rich or poor?"

I'm speechless.

"And, my dear Gretchen, could this be the day, the most important moment you will know, when you finally are awakened to The Answer you've been searching for all your life?"

"I hope so, Simole. Oh, how I hope so."

"It *will* Gretchen… because you've reached *the Mountain*."

My heart pounds with every word she is speaking and races with anticipation with every breath I take, as I listen to words I have never heard spoken before.

Simole lifts her arms and motions to those seated around the table.

"This is my family, and they will help you."

I look around the table, and each face smiles at me.

"Today, you will begin your journey along the Ten Trails of Wisdom.

"Each one here knows his or her trail better than anyone else, and they will be your guide along their trail."

I'm puzzled.

"But Simole, I only see nine people and you said there are *Ten* Trails…."

"Yes, my dear, you are correct. But you must follow all nine trails *before* you reach the tenth. Once you do, it will be *I* who will be your guide along the last, and most important, of all trails."

With a look emanating pure love and compassion, Simole reaches for my hand.

"Smile, my dear Gretchen. For today begins your spiritual journey filled with lessons about Life and about you that will leave you changed forever.

"Lessons the Universe and Great Creator have been waiting to teach you."

And with that, Simole gets up from the table and leaves.

With one last drink of water, I put down my napkin and get up to follow the man who will be my guide as I begin my journey on the first trail.

Chapter 10

THE FIRST TRAIL:
"THE PATH OF PERFECT ORDER"

*M*y guide for the first trail is Simole's nephew, a young man named Cortez.

As we begin our journey, Cortez takes the lead.

"Open your eyes, Ms. Gretchen, for you will see many beautiful things."

As we walk along the footpath through the dense jungle, my eyes keep looking at all the frolicking animals. They are vibrant, active, happy and playful.

Cortez stops as I call his name.

"Cortez, are all the animals in the jungle as playful as these?"

He pauses and smiles as he admires the monkeys playing with each other as they dangle from their tails from a far off thicket of vines.

"They are healthy, happy and living, as Nature intended them to live.

"We are made in the same way; for abundant health and happiness are the will of the Great Creator.

"Look at the animals, Ms. Gretchen. They know nothing of the needless stress of humans. They know not of tomorrow and if food will be found on the nearby vine. But does the uncertainty of the unknown stop their happiness?

"Nature is the great caretaker of all life and gives to all life, without life's ever asking, all the nourishment and sustenance it needs to express itself the way the Great Creator intended."

I let his words sink deeply within me as I continue to observe the perfect order of the plants and trees and flowers and all the other animals of Nature.

I was beginning to realize the importance of this in my life.

For many years, I gave little thought to what I ate, and I felt terrible.

Then, at the times I did feel guilty about not taking better care of myself, I'd overdo it and become some sort of health fanatic, which I quickly grew tired of.

I now began to realize that for too long, I'd been putting other people, things and my job ahead of taking better care of me; it was time to get out of this downward spiral.

As we reach the end of the long trail, Simole is there to greet us.

Cortez bids goodbye as he walks off.

Simole points to a new path ahead of us.

"Come. Shall we walk?

"Tell me Gretchen, of your first, but brief experience on the trail."

"The way the animals played captivated my attention, Simole. They were so happy, so healthy, so vibrant, and so full of life. I only wish I could have a fraction of that much energy."

"Oh, you can, my dear. You can."

I listen closely.

"Everything we do in life depends on our health. The better we feel, the more we can enjoy and experience the bountiful things that life has to offer. For is it not true that when we're healthy, we don't think about our health, yet when we don't feel our best, it's all we think about?"

"It's so true."

"The Great Creator has given each of us a body whose natural state is perfect health. We have everything our body needs to feel its best, if only we'll get out of its way and let Life sustain us."

Simole taps my head gently. "And the way you start feeling better begins with that little marvel here: your brain, my dear."

"Tell me how, Simole."

"Gretchen, your body cannot think.

"It only listens and responds to the commands it is given by what is up here." She touches my head again.

"Those commands are your words, your pictures and your feelings and emotions.

"Now, if your body is designed for perfect health, then why do so many suffer such pain? For as you have just seen on the first trail, is not Life *perfect* order and health?"

"That's how it seems to me."

Simole continues.

"The raw natural resources of the earth Nature has given us are meant for our sustenance and life. Yet, those same resources, when not used as Nature intended, can cause so many of the problems that people experience."

Simole bends down and holds a hand full of leaves and breaks them off to show me as she hands them to me.

"Here, take the coca plant.

"By using its ingredients one way, it gives us herbs that when mixed with others can heal us. Yet use them a different way, and it creates something that can harm us."

I look at it and think how powerful the little plant is.

"You see, Gretchen, many people mistakenly blame illnesses on the Great Creator.

"Oh, but how patient and forgiving the Great Creator is, to listen to so much hurtful talk.

"For, in all the history of man, are not more things that bring us hurt and unhappiness caused by our thoughts than by anything else?"

I beg to differ. "But Simole, c'mon. I've *never* heard of anyone saying worry *killed* someone."

"Ah, Gretchen… is there something called worry that you can hold in your hand and touch?"

"Of course not."

"And that's my point. What happens to the body when they worry doesn't show up in the body or their life as a sickness called worry. No, no, no. Worry disguises itself by becoming diseases that we've given names to."

"So, if our thoughts are as powerful as you say Simole—that they can cause us either perfect health or disease—then how can we keep ourselves in perfect health?"

"Gretchen, would it not help if one looked at one's life with a new set of eyes to see it for what it really is, instead of what we *think* it to be?"

"But how?"

"To do so, we need to step back and first begin by looking at our lives and how we've treated our bodies.

"We will then be enlightened to better understand why we've treated our body as we have.

"Only then can we begin to make the changes our bodies need.

I press for details. "Like what?"

"First, we must give our body those things that are good for it and let go of those things that are not. The body is so forgiving, so resilient, so pliable, and it can very quickly bounce back to its normal perfect health, but not when we bombard it year after year with the things that take its natural wellness away.

"Like stress!"

"Exactly, my dear. Our bodies are much like the plants you see here on the Mountain. Feed and nourish them with food and minerals, bathe them in just the right amount of sunlight and quench them with plenty of life-giving water, and they grow hearty and healthy.

"It's really very simple. We know what we need. We need to listen to the wisdom of our bodies."

Simole pauses.

"The body will tell us what foods make it feel good by giving us the energy and perfect health that is normal for us.

"And when we feel tired with little energy, we must rest and perhaps change the foods we've been eating. This is Nature's call that she needs us to do something different and make those changes."

I jump in. "But Simole, back in the country where I live, it's so easy to be confused with all the magazines, Internet, television and people telling you that you've got to eat this way or follow this new diet or take this weight loss drug or—"

"Gretchen, stop making it so complicated. Just listen to the wisdom of *your* body.

"It will tell you when to eat and when to stop.

"It will tell you when to drink water.

"It will tell you when to sleep and when to awake.

"The body will tell you when too much stress is robbing your happiness and enjoyment from life.

"Your body will tell you *everything* you need to know.

"But if you don't listen to its signals, the body will force you to listen by making you unhappy or sick and keeping you unhappy or sick until you learn to correct your thoughts and actions and once again align them in perfect order with what your body needs.

"Always remember that to enjoy life as the Great Creator intended, we need only follow *The Path of Perfect Order.*"

Chapter 11

THE SECOND TRAIL:
"THE PATH OF THE BODY"

*T*hat afternoon, I'm told, I will travel the second trail and Mariana, Simole's niece, will be my guide.

We meet outside my hut just after lunch. As she leads the way, I'm still excited over what I have learned that morning on the first trail, and I am even more excited wondering what I'm about to discover on this one.

As we journey up the trail, I immediately feel this one is much different than the first.

The terrain is steep and the rocks are jagged. As we ascend, the air is getting thinner.

I gasp, as she is pulling farther away from me.

"Mariana, can we stop and take a breather?"

She stops and turns around and begins walking back down the Mountain to where I stopped.

"Of course. Is everything all right?"

"I thought I was in shape, but this is kickin' my butt…." I hope the "kickin' my butt" part isn't loud enough for her to hear.

"I'm sorry," she says. "Kickin' your…?"

I interrupt. "Whew, this is a very steep mountain. As fast as you're going, you must climb it every day."

"I didn't even realize how fast…. Oh, I'm sorry."

As we sit on a big rock that's half exposed and half buried in the Mountain, I look out over the ravine below and watch as monkeys chase each other up the embankment.

I wipe the sweat from my brow.

"How did you get in *such* good shape?"

"I love to walk, to climb, to run. It makes my body feel so good to be active and moving."

As she is speaking, I realize just how out of shape I am. Sure, I do a few nights of treadmill, bike or stair stepper each week, but it's like I've never done anything at all, now that I'm on the Mountain and putting my in-shape body to the test.

I begin thinking back to the time I was a kid.

All my life, I was a tomboy. Mom would always say I had more energy than a firecracker. Yet, as I got older, more driven and focused, my physical time was gradually replaced with time in the office, time traveling and on the road, time for friends and going out, time for relationships and time for... well, you can fill in the blanks.

Still, there has always been a big part of me that's loved being active, at least more active than I've been.

But sadly, much of my motivation for exercising as of late has gone from fun to necessity, just to keep the pounds off.

We make it up the rest of the Mountain and then work our way down, thank goodness, to the other side.

At the end of the trail, Simole is there to greet us.

Simole is laughing. "Is that sweat I see on your face, or did you run into an unexpected rain shower?"

I look over at Mariana with a thanks-for-pounding-my-tail-in-the-dirt look. "Yeah, I'm pretty beat."

"Come, let's take the easy path back."

Just what I want to hear.

"Tell me Gretchen, what was your experience on the second trail?"

I'm feeling disappointed. "All I know is, I used to be in shape and I can't believe how I've let myself lose it."

"Why be so hard on yourself? Will you not be able to strengthen your body once again?"

"When I get back home I'm going to work out so hard that—"

"And what will you do?"

"What do you mean?"

"To get yourself back into shape?"

"I guess what I've always done. Ride the bike, do the stair stepper, yoga, pilates, run on the treadmill—"

"But do you like doing these things?" she interrupts.

"Yeah, I mean, I *guess* I do. What else would I do? I don't have much time anymore, and I need to do *something* to stay in shape."

"It sounds to me like you're *making* yourself do them."

"Simole, listen. You don't understand. In America, there's a lot of pressure on women to always be thin, to be in shape and to look attractive. I don't like it, and what makes me mad is that so much of the pressure doesn't come from men as much as it does from other women. Simole stops and looks at me. "So why do you care so much what other people think?"

Then the lesson begins.

"Gretchen, just listen to what you say. Why put so much needless pressure on yourself and on your life?

"Look at the animals in the jungle. Do they care what color they are? How fat or thin the other is? How young or old they become?"

"Of course not."

"That's right, my dear. They simply accept what the Great Creator has given them and enjoy their lives as Nature intended.

"Living your life by the fickle and always-changing winds of society or what anyone thinks is a shortcut to unhappiness. And that's what you've been doing, is it not?"

"Yes. You're right, Simole."

"Gretchen, *who* you are and *what* you are, as a most precious creation of the Great Creator, does not depend on *how* you look.

"But… for you to do all the things you want and enjoy, those things do require you to take good care of your body."

We continue walking.

"Just as our good health depends on giving our bodies the right thoughts and nutrients each day, the body is the most marvelous of all machines and must be used every day for it to work its best.

"If we take care of our body, it will take care of us.

"One of the laws of life and for the body is that either *we use it or we lose it.*

"Actually, we truly have no idea what our body is capable of, for we've never reached the limit of knowing everything it can do.

"Mentally, we know of no limits of our brains; and once we reach the end of our present knowledge, we always find that a whole new world of knowledge opens up for us to learn.

"That is its beauty.

"Life is constantly expanding to express itself and continues to do so without limit."

I interrupt.

"Simole, I feel like I want to do so much more with my life and feel that I can, but I just don't know how or what to do."

Simole motions and points to a spot under a large tree for us to sit down.

"Gretchen, first you need exercise. Not too much and not too little. You just need some type of exercise each day and it should be exercise you *enjoy* and *never* feel forced to do.

"Life is all about movement. And the more movement we have, the more life we experience."

"But Simole, how does one know what exercise to do and for how long?"

"It's simple. Find the kind of exercise that makes *you* feel good, makes your heart beat and your lungs move, and makes you breathe deeply and makes your body sweat. Then do it until your body *tells* you it's had enough. Then stop and give the body rest."

"Can it be *that* simple?"

Simole smiles.

"Yes. It *is* that simple.

"But there's more.

44

"The body needs new and different things, so don't allow it to grow tired by doing the same thing over and over.

"Our life is exciting in proportion to the number of things we have to look forward to. And the more new and different ways you move your body, by doing something *a little different* every day, the more you'll be greatly rewarded."

I'm smiling, thinking about just how fun this is going to be once I get back to New York City.

"Remember this, Gretchen: Give your body the exercise you love, the kind your body enjoys, and you will always be able to follow *The Path of the Body* wherever and whatever trail you are on in your life."

Chapter 12

THE THIRD TRAIL:
"THE PATH OF THE GREAT CREATOR"

*L*ater that same afternoon, a steady rain pelts the jungle with one of the many daily showers so common this time of year.

As I'm sitting and relaxing in a bamboo chair that envelops my body, Casteda, Simole's younger brother, appears in the clearing in front of me and hurriedly motions.

"Come, Ms. Gretchen. We must not miss it."

I hurriedly hop toward him while trying to slip my shoes on.

"What, Casteda? Miss what?"

"Come, you'll see."

Quickly we follow a new trail I've never seen—thank heavens it's flat—and we make our way to the back side.

There, in front of me, is a great river below.

As the rain has now stopped, we sit down on the side of the Mountain.

A large towering tree releases droplets of water off its leaves and onto our heads and makes a rhythmic, soothing pitter-patter on the ground around us.

Casteda is smiling and pointing, motioning me to look to my far right.

Off in the distance is the most breathtaking rainbow I've ever seen.

Wide ribbons of magnificent colors are painted across the horizon as if the Great Painter dipped His brush and wiped it across the canvas of sky.

But there is more.

As Casteda looks down, he raises his hand and points to the left.

On the other side of the rainbow, as if it began from the water, an incredible blue mist of steam rises from the tranquil waters, almost like someone has poured hot water over ice. The steam mixes with the colors of the rainbow to create a surreal sight that I thought could be found only in paintings.

This is indeed the work of the Great Painter; the Great Artist that Michelangelo, Titian, Degas, Picasso and all the others learned from.

The animals, plants, birds and all of Nature I was experiencing, and now this, gives me pause.

For this—for the first time in my life—is inspiring me in ways I never expected with a thought that keeps playing in my head… for *all that I had seen* spoke to me to perhaps trust more in the Great Creator for *all that I had not seen*.

I am moved beyond words.

As we watch in amazement while the rainbow fades from the sky, but not from my mind, Simole quietly walks up and joins us. "It's always beautiful."

I sigh. "Oh… I wish I'd had my camera so I could've taken pictures to remember this moment."

"A camera could not capture what you see and feel, my dear Gretchen."

She gently taps my head.

"The only camera you need is right here."

We all pause once more to see the final curtain call of this day's show.

"Come, let's walk back and talk."

We begin our walk.

"Gretchen, tell me of what you just experienced."

"Simole, I know I saw a rainbow, but I felt something more, something deeper, something that I've never felt before."

"Yes.... Please, go on."

"For the first time in my life, I felt close to, as you would say, the Great Creator. Does that make any sense?"

"Perfect sense, my dear. Tell me of this feeling."

I pause. "It's like in a flash of the moment, something inside me was awakened. Something *big*. Something *deep* that I never knew existed before."

There's a moment of silence. Then, before she can answer, I blurt, "Oh, just forget it. It doesn't mean anything."

"Never make excuses for the things you feel, Gretchen. For the Great Creator would not have given you those feelings unless It meant for you to use them to help you and guide you."

She then motions for us to stop.

"Come. Let's sit here. I have something to say that you are now ready to hear."

My eyes lock into hers.

"Many people in life never experience what you just have, because they won't *let* themselves."

"What do you mean, Simole?"

"Gretchen, when the Universe calls us, it's time for us to listen. And It is always communicating with us, if only we'll stop and hear the message.

"One doesn't have to live in a big city like you do, Gretchen, to know how many things around us we miss seeing, hearing and understanding simply because of the busyness of our lives.

"Yet, in only a few moments here on this trail on the Mountain, you took the time to stop, look and listen to what your heart is telling you, did you not?"

I think for a moment and nod in agreement.

"Look at how many of our lives are so filled with *us* that we have no time to hear the Universe calling our name."

"Simole, it's so true."

"Gretchen, let me ask you a question. How many times have you traveled the same way to home or work, only to find that on one day, you saw something that was always there along your path, but you had never noticed it before?"

I think for a moment. "I do remember times like that, when I traveled down the same way each day, and one day, I saw something different and thought to myself that I had never seen that before."

"Yet it was always there waiting for you to discover it, wasn't it?"

"Yes, it was."

She continues.

"Do you think that perhaps the reason you didn't notice it before was because of how much your thoughts were on the little things and distractions that kept your head full of endless conversations you have with yourself, that you keep replaying over and over, every day?

"Day after day, you kept missing those things, until one day your mind opened just a tiny bit more, let in just a little more light, let in a little more room for something different and new and, perhaps, even something inspiring?"

I smile.

"You see, Dear One, the Universe is always calling our name, if only we will listen.

"The Universe knows what we need and when we need it.

"The Universe knows the right way and best way we need to travel to lead us to all that we dream of and desire.

"But to hear Its call, we must keep a part of our heart always open to receive Its message and then follow the path, our own path, It tells us to take."

"But how can I do that, living the incredibly crazy busy life I have and living in the concrete jungle of Manhattan among millions of people?"

"Gretchen, first, you must listen.

"To take a few moments each day just to sit, listen and observe, just like you've done here in the jungle.

"Even in New York, whenever and wherever you are, pause for a moment and just watch, without judging what you see, the cars, taxis, buses and people go by.

"Take your mind off of yourself, and that's the moment the Universe will talk to you. You see, inspiration can be found any-where, at any time, if only we'll be open to receive it.

"The desire inside you to grow, to experience and to become what you dream of is the will of the Universe. For you are a living extension of the Universe. You are a piece of the Divine; and by your dreams and desires, your life grows and expands, and at the same time so does the Universe."

"C'mon, Simole. You're telling me that of the all the billions of people on this planet, that whatever it is that created me, really cares about what I'm doing or wanting? I really find that hard to believe."

Simole pauses for a moment and looks at me with great seriousness.

"Gretchen. This thing you feel, this desire deep down inside of you that keeps calling you, is the Universe seeking to release and express itself through you.

"Ever wonder why you have the talents you have, the dreams you have, or why the personality you have is unlike any of the other billions of people?"

I stop and consider the enormity of what Simole has just said. "Wow… that's huge. Billions of people, and yet each of us is unique"

Simole grins. "Just *that* alone should tell you just how impor-tant you are to this planet, to those around you and to this power we call Life.

"One never knows when or how the Universe will call us, but as sure as you are sitting next to me and breathing the air of life on this mountain right now, the Universe will breathe new life into you, if only you'll *let* it."

I look around at all the trees, plants and animals that surround us, and I'm more amazed now at what I'm seeing. Perhaps Simole's words are opening my mind to let more of what's around me to enter inside.

I look over at her. "Simole, I wish my family and friends could experience what I'm experiencing right now."

Simole puts her arm around me as we get up and begin our walk again. "My dear, they will *never* understand how *you* feel.

"They will never understand how what you've just experienced changed something inside of *you*.

"And you know what? That's okay."

I let her words sink in.

It really *is* okay. I don't need to convince others why I do the things I do or feel the way I feel. They've got their feelings and lives, and I've got mine. It's time for me to release any and everyone from my life and just let them be whoever and whatever they are.

I'm feeling a sense of freedom and relief that I've never known, and Simole is sensing it. She starts to laugh. "You look like the weight of the world has been lifted from your shoulders, my dear."

"It feels like it, Simole. I'm tired of thinking so much about what others think about me."

"Good for you, Dear One. Good for you!"

We continue our walk as we quietly observe the jungle around us.

"Gretchen, it's time to begin trusting yourself again.

"Be careful of those who say they know the best way for you to live your life. For they may know the way for *them*, but unless they have *your* soul, have lived inside *your* body, have *your* same dreams and have experienced all the emotions *you* feel the *same* way *you* feel them, then how is it that anyone can say they know what's best for *you*?"

I nod; she's right.

"Here, on the Mountain, Life teaches us many lessons. The Great Creator is never found only within the boxes or labels we try to put It in.

"Tell me, Gretchen; being here on the Mountain and experiencing the wonder of Life and of Nature, do you feel a connection to the Power that created all you can see?"

Without hesitation I say, "I do Simole. I really do."

"Then look around us, dear Gretchen, and *this time* I want you to see something that you've been missing." Simole pauses for a few seconds. "Do you see it?"

I look, but I don't see anything. "See what, Simole?"

"You mean you don't see lack and limitation or worry, doubt and fear?"

"Of course not, Simole."

"That's because those things come from humans, Gretchen.

"The Great Creator knows nothing of lack and limitation or worry and fear.

"All It knows is unlimited abundance and expression.

"Look at the magnificence of the stars, the moon, the universe and the sun; the unstoppable power of the oceans, the change of seasons, how night follows day; the unchanging laws of gravity, the rising and setting of the sun each day without fail.

"And look at us, a tiny speck in this great cosmos of Life. But each of us tiny specks here for a reason, with a purpose and a calling and desire to experience.

"*Keep your mind focused more on the possibilities and less on the problems and your life will change dramatically.*

"Nothing in this life is so great that it will ever break your spirit. Remember that.

"Never give in to adversity and hardship, no matter how hard things may be at the time.

"Begin to see such things as your friends and your teachers, who are in your life at that moment to help you learn the lesson

Life wants to teach you, so you may grow and become more, with a fresh, new, higher level of awareness and understanding.

"And with each lesson you learn and each experience you have, you become of aware of brand new possibilities for expressing yourself in ways you never dreamed possible."

I begin feeling better, hearing Simole's encouragement.

"Simole, I have already experienced what you are talking about. Whenever I've gone through something painful in my life, I've always found a way to get through it; and after some time has passed, it gets much easier for me to look back at the experience and realize what I learned from it and how it helped me grow."

Simole is pleased at what she hears me say.

"Yes, my dear one. We all have experienced the same as you.

"And one of the most wonderful things about this Life is that, each time a new lesson is learned, the old part of us that was used for teaching us the lesson passes, and in its place is born a new part of us, ready and able to learn the next lesson.

"A shedding of the old, to make room for new.

"This is the desire of Life: for you to grow, to learn, to love, as your journey takes you along *The Path of the Great Creator,* wherever it may lead you."

Chapter 13

THE FOURTH TRAIL: "THE PATH OF NATURE'S FLOW"

The next morning, my journey to the fourth trail is to begin.

After another bountiful breakfast at Simole's, filled also with much laughter and good conversation, Mastina, Simole's younger sister, is introduced as my guide.

As everyone bids us goodbye, we leave for the 15-minute walk to the beginning of the trail.

Once on the trail, I notice that this, among all the other trails, has a much different type of vegetation and terrain; it's sparse and more exposed to sun, making it drier than the lush greenery I was used to seeing by now.

As we make our way down the trail to a clearing, Mastina points to a flat spot inclined between a group of rocks.

We take our seats and remain quiet.

After a few minutes of silent sitting and watching, I lean over to Mastina and whisper, "What are we looking for?"

Mastina raises her hand and puts her index finger close to her lips. "Shhh...."

A few minutes go by and she raises her hand again, this time pointing in front of us.

Out from beneath a bush comes what appears to be a large iguana.

I whisper back. "It's beautiful."

She points to a group of field mice rummaging close by and murmurs, "Watch closely."

As the iguana watches, the field mice stop and take notice, then determine all is safe and continue to rollick around.

But all is not safe.

The iguana begins to change color, albeit subtly, until it blends in perfectly with the surroundings. If my eyes hadn't been glued to it as I watched the transformation, I would've easily missed it. It's not an iguana, I thought. It's a chameleon.

As the chameleon slowly inches closer and closer to the mice, I know what's about to happen. Suddenly, as one of the mice wanders off and is now close to the chameleon's face, the chameleon lashes out like a whip and holds the mouse in its mouth and trots off.

Mastina looks over at me with a whisper. "Things are never what they may first appear to be."

I listen to her words and pause, as the sight of the chameleon and mouse makes me think of some of the things in my life that aren't what they appear to be.

As long as I can remember, I've always been the kind of person who wanted control.

Control of my life.

Control of events.

Control of knowing what was going to happen before I did it.

And for more years than I care to count, I've been constantly frustrated.

Early on, I was the one who believed in the goodness in everybody; the one who would take people at their word. If they told me they'd help me or that things would get done, I'd believe them.

Sadly, many times things didn't turn out quite like they said.

So I started to become cynical of people, of life, of relationships and of myself and ability or lack thereof to trust.

I didn't like who I was becoming; my nature had always been to trust, but with so many "chameleons" I had run into, I knew of no other way.

Mastina rises and motions to me that it's time to go.

As we leave our spectator section on the Mountain, Simole is waiting for us at the end of the trail.

"You look a little surprised, Gretchen."

"Animal nature and human nature are sometimes too similar for me."

"How so?"

"Well Simole, watching what I first thought to be an iguana, which turned out to be really a chameleon, and watching how the mice first thought so too, then seeing the chameleon become something different…"

"Was not the chameleon a chameleon all along?"

"Yes; I mean watching the chameleon disguise itself and its true intentions to the mice, really opened my eyes to a lot of things."

We begin our walk back.

"It's time to tell me of them."

"For so long now, Simole, I've believed so many things that I thought were the way I believed they were, only to find out that they weren't.

"I've believed too many people for too long. I've been lied to, deceived, used and humiliated in my relationships, with so-called 'friends' and in my career.

"Why have I been so gullible and now have turned into someone so jaded and hard-edged; someone I really don't like?"

As we continue walking, Simole takes a detour.

"Come, I want to show you something."

As we cut a new jungle path, we stop about 100 feet off the trail.

She points to a small garden plot.

"Look at this, Gretchen, and tell me what you see."

"I see a garden."

"Is that all you see? Look closely."

I scout it over.

"Well… I see on one end, some beautiful flowers growing…"

"And on the other end?"

"I don't see flowers, I see weeds."

"Very good." She turns to walk back.

Huh? Was that all? That was too easy; there had to be more to it than that.

"Simole."

"Yes?"

"The garden we looked at back there…"

"Yes?"

"Why did you show it to me?"

"Gretchen, just as the chameleon you saw was not the chameleon you thought or what the mice expected, neither are our lives when we believe all those chameleons in our minds we've created by the seeds we have planted."

"What do you mean?"

"Your deeper mind is like the most rich and fertile soil you can imagine, and it will grow *anything* you plant in it. But… *you* must first plant something, or else weeds will grow."

"*I* must plant something?"

"Yes. *You* must be the planter and no on else.

"What you think and what you believe about yourself, your family, friends, your job, your relationships and life are like seeds.

"If you think positive and happy thoughts, you plant seeds that will bring you flowers in your garden.

"If you keep thinking negatively, you plant weeds that will choke off and kill the flowers.

"And unless you daily go to your garden and get rid of the weeds, the flowers in your life that you want to grow will never bloom."

I stop for a moment and blurt out loud.

"Rid the weeds and my life will bloom."

Simole stops and looks over at me with her reassuring smile. "Oh yes, my dear.

"Gretchen, your garden doesn't care *what* you plant in it, for it will grow weeds just as easily as it will grow flowers.

"It is *you,* Gretchen, it is *you* alone who can decide what *you* will plant in your garden.

"And only *you* will pick the harvest from planting the *right* seeds in your garden."

"I never understood it quite like that before, Simole. I never knew..."

"The truth is, we don't *know* the truth about ourselves.

"The things we believe about who we are, what other people or things are, are greatly influenced and molded early in life by our parents, family, friends and society, and they continue to be formed during the rest of our lives.

"That is, unless *we* take control of *our* thoughts and emotions and direct them the way *we* choose.

"The Great Creator gave us but one power over which you, and no one else, will ever have complete control. Do you know what that power is?"

I stop walking to pause and think for a moment.

Simole answers. "It's the power of your thoughts.

"Now, I ask you, if The Great Creator believed that such ability was so important, what does that tell you about how that power can change your life?"

"I've never really stopped to think about the things I think about, Simole."

Simole chuckles.

"Oh my dear, most haven't either, so you're in good company."

I laugh. "But I don't know if I still want to be in such good company."

Simole is smiling. "Then start thinking *differently.*"

Simole quickly walks ahead of me. "Come... look over here."

She is pointing to a running brook swirling a pool of water off to its side. I look down and watch it.

"Nature continues to fill that pool of water, doesn't it?" she asks.

"Yes, it does."

Simole bends down to grab a fallen twig and hands it to me.

"Take this twig, Gretchen, and dig around the edges of the pool of water."

I bend down and start moving the stick back and forth.

"That's it! Go ahead and make the pool of water bigger…keep making it bigger!"

With each time the twig digs into the earth, water immediately fills the hole.

"Do you see what is happening?"

"No matter how hard, how big, or how long you dig, Nature is immediately filling any mold you give it."

She pauses. "And the same thing happens in our lives every minute of every day."

"What do you mean?"

"Our thoughts, our beliefs about who we are and what we believe we're worthy to receive—be it money, health, happiness, love or anything else—each creates a mold that Life fills by our *expectations* of what we *believe* we are worthy to experience.

"Life never plays favorites and does not listen to how much you hope or beg for things to be different. It is up to *you* to change your thoughts and beliefs to *make* them different. *That's* how you get rid of the chameleons in your life."

I keep swirling the stick and watching the water fill the new holes I am digging.

Simole continues. "You see, Life is completely neutral, as the Great Creator so lovingly made it to be, and It will give you as much or as little as you *believe* you should have.

"For those beliefs become the mold that Life will fill; and make no mistake, my dear one, Life *always* answers and fills the mold *you* give it."

Of all the experiences I've had and lessons learned thus far, I think this is the one that's hitting me the hardest.

As I'm still bending down and swirling the stick in the water, I look up at her.

"Simole, I want to change my life. I've wanted to for years, but I've been afraid and confused, and I don't know how. What must I do? Can... can you tell me how?"

I get up and drop the stick as she puts her arm around my shoulder and pulls me closer as we begin walking.

"To begin our journey, we must first be cleansed of our wrong thinking.

"Realize that you don't have all the answers and you never will in just one lifetime. No one will. And that's okay.

"In this life, we learn as we go, and if we make a decision we don't like, we can change it at any time and make a better decision. The choice is and will be always ours.

"As we begin our cleansing, we must first begin to treat ourselves with compassion and stop being so demanding and hard on ourselves. Life doesn't expect this from anyone. We need to see our lives and those in it in a different way."

"How Simole?"

"Gretchen, let me tell you a story...

"Many years ago, a man visited the Mountain and told me a story I have never forgotten. A worldly traveler, this man told of how his experience at The Louvre changed his life.

"One day, he said, as he walked through room after room filled with thousands of paintings from the world's greatest masters, his immediate urge was to stand close to the priceless masterpieces, almost as if to touch them and the mark they have left on humanity.

"But as he moved closer and closer, he noticed something that disturbed him. The clarity, beauty and crispness of the paintings he admired from a distance began to blur, for he could now only see the chips, fading, flaws and mistakes on the canvas.

"Yet as soon as he began to take one step backward, then another, and another, away from the painting, he no longer saw the flaws and mistakes.

"They had now disappeared, and the crispness, detail, beauty and breathtaking magnificence of the masterpiece returned in its splendor.

"The same is true of the jungle, the plants, the animals and all other things in it.

"Stand too close, and you see the flaws and miss all the other beauty that surrounds it.

"But stand back and see it as it's meant to be seen, and your heart is filled with awe.

"Gretchen, when you look too closely at yourself, your life and those in it, it's too easy to see the imperfections and flaws in them and ourselves. This only takes away from the joy in our hearts.

"Yet, when you stand back and see the beauty and see life and yourself from a distance, happiness can then flood your heart and soul, as you realize that you and everyone around you, truly are divine masterpieces, created by the greatest Master of them all, on the canvas we call Life."

I stop and let her words soak in, and I realize just how critical I've been of others, of life and myself.

Simole sees me thinking and pauses a few more seconds before she begins again.

"Gretchen, like the child we once were, and have never stopped being, we must start *trusting* Life again."

"But that can be scary."

"Yes, but look at what working so hard at having control over all the things in your life has brought to you, Gretchen."

"Geez… a whole lot of unhappiness, worry and frustration."

Simole nods.

"We may plan and work diligently toward whatever we want, but Life has its own timing and flow.

"How we get into the flow and right timing for our lives is when we let our dreams and desires go to the Great Creator, our Higher Power within, and *trust that It will bring us not always that which we want, but that which we need for our greatest joy and happiness.*

"Start being good to yourself once again, and let yourself enjoy the masterfully choreographed play of how your life unfolds each day."

I shake my head. "It might be tough for me to do at first, Simole, but I'm going to give it a try and do it."

"I know you will." Simole continues, "So let me ask you a question, Gretchen."

"Sure, go ahead."

"Does your work fill you with passion?"

I think for a moment. "Hmm… Well, I like what I'm doing, but I can't say I'm *passionate* about it."

"Then why do you keep doing it?"

"Because I'm good at it. I work with some great people. It pays great money. I get to travel. And I've got benefits and job security."

"Does that sound like the answers you'd hear from someone whose work gives them life, energy, enthusiasm and passion?"

I shake my head.

"No, not really."

"Gretchen, the world is full of human robots that day after day, year after year, go to jobs they dislike, do the tasks that are unfulfilling, and come home to forget about it all, only to wake up and do it all again.

"The great majority of people don't really know what they truly want out of Life. And since they don't take the time to think about what it is that would bring them happiness, they accept other people's definition of success and will work precious year after precious year of their lives—all to achieve something they really didn't want in the first place."

"I know a lot of people like that, Simole."

"Perhaps you know one of them better than you thought."

She's talking about me. She says, "Show me where is it written that one must suffer through great unhappiness in this life, by doing anything one doesn't love, just for sake of fear, avoiding ridicule, owning more things, a bigger bank account or for some reward when the candle of our lives has been blown out.

"All you have, my dear Gretchen, is this life, this moment, this day. And you would be among the wisest of all people if you remember that.

"Begin *this* moment to live as you so deeply *desire*.

"Live in the moment and let that moment, carry you to the next great moment."

I love that. *Live in the moment and let that moment, carry you to the next great moment.*

"Think about the people whom you admire most. Are they not passionate about their lives? Are they not filled with energy, power, strength, vitality and a commitment to use their given talents to touch, in some way, the lives of others?"

"It's true, Simole. Those who have inspired me have been those who lived their lives with enthusiasm and passion."

Simole smiles. "Can I tell you a secret? That same passion is inside of you right now."

"You really think so, Simole?"

"Oh, yes. And it doesn't come when all your bills are paid, or you have more money in the bank or if you have the right mate or move to a new city.

"Your passion is waiting for you to use it right now.

"And here's the best news of all: By doing so, in the work you love doing, you become filled with enthusiasm and the power of a wildfire, and are able to touch the lives of those all around you and those whom you may never know.

"And Gretchen?"

"Yes, Simole?"

"We become the people we admire the most."

"That's something I want, Simole; it really is."

"Then begin by always trusting your emotions. They are the most powerful guiding force that the Great Creator has put inside of you. Listen to your emotions and trust them, Gretchen, and you'll never go astray.

"Follow the passion inside of you and give Life a bigger mold to fill, for it can fill any dream you give it.

"It's time to plant only flowers in your garden.

"That will keep you always in *The Path of Nature's Flow.*"

Chapter 14

THE FIFTH TRAIL: "THE PATH OF THE CARETAKER"

*T*he afternoon sun rises high in the sky as its light bolts dance through the trees.

Tops of leaves glisten as they are kissed by the warmth of its light. This afternoon, we are journeying along the fifth trail, and Luis, Simole's cousin, is my guide.

As we begin along the crooked path, his eyes seem to catch every movement in the jungle.

It's easy to see how much Luis loves the rainforest, especially to observe his kindred spirit for the animals who call it home.

Luis asks me to stop.

Above us, some 150 feet or so in the trees is a loud rustling and commotion in the branches.

He points upward.

"Up there, Ms. Gretchen. Look."

Our heads tilt to the sky.

"What is it, Luis?"

"It's time for the baby eagle to leave its nest, and it doesn't want to."

"What happens if it doesn't leave?"

He laughs. "Oh, the mother will push it out."

I'm not getting the humor in it.

"But Luis, is the young bird ready to leave? Won't it die?"

"Oh no, Ms. Gretchen. Nature has made the choice, and the time has come for Nature to take over, for it's given the young bird all the ability it will ever need to survive. Now it has no choice but to use it or die."

"How cruel."

Luis reassures me.

"Just being kicked out of the nest won't hurt the bird. Just watch, for it will quickly forget it's been a baby as it becomes an eagle."

As I sit watching this rite of passage for such a young creature, Luis's words sink deep.

Here is this creature that has lived more by instinct than by choice; and regardless of the decision its parents or Nature made, the odds are stacked in its favor that it will survive.

And here I am, a creation of the same Great Creator, but with one big difference; I have the power of choice in my life.

I start to think how different my life could be if I would start using more of that power to change things in my life that for too long have needed changing.

As Luis and I make our way along the trail, having watched another similar ritual, this time by a taper and its young, I was amazed to have witnessed such a rare event as these two, on this day, on this mountain.

At the end of the trail, like clockwork, Simole, dressed in a brick colored dress and sandals, greets us with those warm brown eyes and that sweet loving smile as the wind tosses back her flowing locks of silvery hair.

This time, with a big beaming smile, I am the first to speak. "Simole, I think I'm starting to get the hang of this lesson-learning thing on each new trail."

"Well, let's hear."

"I think what we just witnessed was Nature at its best. The power of instinct and without anything or anyone telling it, how the eagle and the taper knew it was time to make their young survive on their own."

"And how did such a sight affect you, may I ask?"

"Simole, I think the bird and animal had no choice. Their destiny was decided for them. And despite how much they may have squawked and how hard it was at first for me to hear and watch what was happening, I knew they would survive, they would make it, and they would continue to do what Nature intended for them to do."

Simole is hoping I will see the lesson for my life. "And what about you, Gretchen?"

"I think seeing all that helped me realize that I have the power to decide. I have the power of choice; and I'm ashamed to admit this, but I haven't been using it like I could."

I ramble on. "Sure, I have survived, and to most people, it looks like I've done really well for myself. But, I've been more like that bird than a human."

"Tell me how so?"

"It's like I've almost been on autopilot, doing whatever I thought I needed to do to get ahead and achieve all the things I thought would bring me happiness and fulfillment; but I've been wrong."

"You really think so?"

I pause and try to forget about it. "What am I doing complaining? What about all those people who have no choices in their lives? What about them?"

Simole is about to set me straight.

"Gretchen, will you not agree that many people in life have families that have been blessings while others seem like a curse?"

"Of course."

Simole looks off into the jungle. "For how is it that Life treats us fairly when one comes from a family of love and the other comes from one of abuse and neglect?"

"Exactly!"

"But, Gretchen, it's not Life that did the choosing."

"What do you mean, Simole?"

"We must understand that everyone in life is given only one power that no one can or will ever be able to take away from them, and it is the power of choosing how to live and what to believe."

I'm still somewhat confused. "But what about people who live in oppressed conditions? They didn't ask to live like that, did they?"

She challenges me. "Let me ask you, have not other people in the world that lived in those same conditions, escaped to find a better life?"

"Of course, Simole."

"So, what you're saying then, is they had a choice to either stay or go, change their lives or keep living them the same? Would this be correct?"

"Yes, they did have a choice, and they made a decision to change things."

"And did they not *always* have that power inside of them to change, and one day came and it was *finally* the day they *decided* to use it?"

"Hmm…"

"If a man abandons his family, has he not made a choice?"

"Yes."

"If a woman loves her family, has she not made an equally powerful choice?"

"Of course."

"Gretchen, we must understand that abuse, neglect, or doing things that cause us harm rest solely on the shoulders of the person making the choice and on no one or nothing else. It is never anyone else's fault that *they* are the reason this person chose the actions, experiences, and results of those actions in their lives."

It was all beginning to make sense.

"Now, the statement you have made about all those people who, as you say, have no choices, let's talk about that."

I opened the can of worms now.

"What about the person who was raised in such a difficult environment. What can they do to overcome such seeming lack, hardship and unfairness?"

"Think differently?"

"Very good, my dear!"

"We must understand that Life is always fair and their future unhappiness or happiness will be because of *either* the choice they make of *choosing to accept* the same kind of life of the parent or parents or loved one that's caused them so much pain, or by *making a different choice not to accept* those beliefs, actions and experiences.

"Gretchen, they do so by thinking the opposite thoughts and of doing the opposite things in their lives that their parent or parents chose not to do in theirs. It's that easy."

"Come on Simole, you make it sound so simple."

"Gretchen, it *is* simple. Think about it: Regardless of whether you're a woman or man, is not life a *choice,* and is it not the choices each of us makes that determine the *results* we get and the experiences we have?"

I contemplate for a moment. "Yes."

"Then, if something's not working in our life or if it's bringing us unhappiness, we must first examine our own thoughts and actions of *why* we chose those beliefs and actions in the first place, why we are still keeping them; and then we must change them, and *keep changing them,* until we get the results we want.

"Gretchen, do you remember the baby eagle that you saw?"

"Yes, seeing it was both beautiful and eye-opening."

"That baby eagle and its mother can teach you a powerful lesson and it is this: *Life changes the moment you realize.*

"When a young eagle is born, it can barely move. The mother must make sure her baby is fed and protected from predators.

"Quickly, the eagle grows and gets stronger until one day, the eagle flaps its wings and leaves the nest and begins to soar high in the sky.

"The eagle was born with everything it would need to become the most majestic of birds and the most respected of predators in the sky.

"Everything the eagle would or could ever need, the seeds for its greatness, was given to it at birth.

"Those seeds lay asleep inside until one day, and with a little help from its mother, the eagle *realizes* its greatness and ability and *awakens* those seeds by leaving the comfort and familiarity of the nest to become what the Universe calls it to become—the most majestic of all birds.

"Gretchen, *you* are just like the eagle."

"Simole, do you really think so? Too often I don't feel like it."

"Oh, yes you are, Gretchen. Oh, yes you are. When you were born, *everything* that you would ever need to achieve and experience in this life, *anything* your heart desired, was given to you.

"And all of these years, those seeds have lain asleep inside of you, *waiting* for the day you finally awake and *realize* just what potential and power you have and how magnificent you are.

"Most importantly, *everything* you will *ever* need to achieve *any* dreams in your heart and have the kind of life you so deeply desire, is inside of you *right now,* waiting for you to *realize* this; for as soon as you do, you begin to immediately *release* its power in your life.

"For the more you realize and accept your greatness and how magnificent the Universe created you to be, the more you will understand that you hold the keys to any kind of life you desire.

"Yes, the Universe is waiting, and has been waiting your whole life, for this moment. It's time to answer its call."

I stop on the trail we are walking and gaze out upon all the beauty of the jungle.

Simole's words have lit a spark inside me.

She sees how much of an impact her words are having on me as she gently takes my hands and looks at me.

"Gretchen, my dear, Life will support us in any decision we make.

"If we choose to rise above our hurts, our anger, our fears, doubts and worries, we have then chosen to thrive and not just survive. Doing so will put us back into the flow of blessings that Life wants to give us.

"For Life is *always* our best friend, partner and guide and will *always* provide for all of our needs.

"We simply need to trust It as It leads us down the right road… along *The Path of the Caretaker.*"

Chapter 15

THE SIXTH TRAIL: "THE PATH OF THE FLOWING RIVER"

*T*he third day has arrived, and time is clicking off faster than I could have imagined.

In two days, I've traveled along five trails and learned more about Nature, Life and myself than could fill the pages of my nightstand diary.

This morning, the air is cool and crisp as the morning dew drips from the trees.

Before I left the garden last night, Simole told me that Guillermina, her granddaughter, would be my guide. Guillermina is the youngest of her grandchildren and the one who best understands the animals of the jungle.

Guillermina and I start our trek on the sixth trail right after breakfast. As we enter the trail, Guillermina speaks to me about her passion. "The rainforest is filled with more animals, plants, birds and insects than man knows about, even after all these years.

"Ever since I was a child, I loved animals. Each day I would come into the jungle and play, try to swing like the monkeys off tree limbs, jump creek banks like the deer and run and tumble down the soft hillside until my little body was so tired I had to rest.

"The animals would always watch from a distance, almost as if they knew what I was doing and—"

She stops talking.

A spotted fawn and her mother appear from behind a thicket of bushes and stop.

Guillermina points her palm to the ground behind her for me to stop.

Without making a sound and doing the best I can to be as still as rock, the deer slowly take small steps towards us.

The mother leads, and the baby follows a few steps behind.

Guillermina slowly holds out both hands, showing the mother doe her palms.

The deer move closer until they stop about two feet in front of her.

The mother sniffs and snorts, as the top of her spotted tail quickly moves from side to side and then up and down, exposing the all-white fur underneath.

The baby comes closer and stands next to its mother.

The mother, with ears down, sticks out her neck toward Guillermina's hands and starts slowly licking her palms.

Guillermina slowly turns her head back ever so slightly to look my way.

I'm smiling.

She makes eye contact with me and then moves her eyes to the deer quickly and then again to me, as if to silently say, "Be still; she'll come to you, too."

I wait.

The mother moves a step, then another, to Guillermina's right and towards me.

Not wanting to frighten it, I slowly raise my right arm up from my side and stretch it out to her.

She quickly snorts, raises her tail and moves back, with the baby turning and quickly jumping away a few feet.

I stand motionless.

In a few seconds, the mother comes closer as her sniffer works overtime.

As she drops her head and ears, her nose inches closer, as air from it blows against the skin of my palm.

Her mouth opens slightly and out comes her tongue, giving my fingers the wildest of baths they've ever had.

For chrissakes, where's my phone!

A few moments go by and the deer quickly turn away, and in a flash they hop out of sight over the next hill.

I'm amazed. "Wow! I've never had *that* happen before."

Guillermina smiles.

"Moments like that are rare. It's like Nature says, 'Here's a little surprise for you to remember.'"

"Guillermina, where is the baby's father?"

"Oh, deer don't have families like we do. The buck, the male deer, will only follow the doe for a few weeks during the period of the year when she is ready to be bred."

"And then what happens?"

"Well, the female will have the baby and be close to it and raise it until it is old enough to go out on its own."

I look up at a group of monkeys sitting high in the branches of some trees.

"That seems too cold to me."

I point to them.

"What about the monkeys? Is it the same for them too?"

"Oh no Gretchen. The monkeys have mates who will stay with them for life. That is their family, and they stay with the family to raise the young and have more young. And unless they are mean and do something terrible and are chased away by the older and bigger males, the babies stay with them as they get older too."

Some *Animal Planet* junkie I thought I was.

As we stop for a rest and a little relaxation under the shade of the draped leaves of a flowering tree, I begin thinking about my life and all the friends and relationships I've had.

Many have come and gone, and far fewer have remained. I guess they were right, whoever said, "At the end of your life, consider yourself lucky if you can count the number of true friends on one hand and really lucky if it takes two."

A half hour later, we make it to the end of the trail, and Simole's there to greet us, carrying a flask of water.

She hands me the flask.

"Welcome back. Care for a cool drink?"

I twist the top off and take four big swigs and wipe off the open end with my T-shirt before handing it over to Guillermina.

We begin walking, as Guillermina drinks, hands the flask back to Simole and then waves as she walks away from us.

"So, my dear, will you tell me of your experience?"

"Simole, there are two things that impress me about what I just saw."

"I'd like to hear about them."

"The first was how such wild animals can be so curious about what they see. I mean, the mother and baby deer couldn't take their eyes off of Guillermina and me, and they even came close enough to touch us. They didn't know who or what we were, but we could have been predators and harmed them. That surprised me."

Simole smiles as she lets out a gentle "Ahh" and begins.

"Gretchen, to watch the animals in the jungle can teach us many things.

"We are reminded that we, too, were once like them, ever exploring new and different things without reason or giving a thought to what others were thinking, or what surprises were waiting for us ahead.

"Look at how curious the mother and her fawn were. Something inside of them urged them to follow their curiosity, did it not?"

"Absolutely."

"You see my dear, as we grow older in years, so do many of us in spirit, for our childlike curiosity is no longer something to be admired, but that which is to be silenced and even feared.

"For, friends, family and the world in which we live, all became convinced at some point in each of their lives—and mistakenly so—that *to find security in life is something far greater to possess than to find happiness.*

"A kind of happiness that only curiosity can bring.

"But so few ever realize that the time we find security in our lives is the moment we give up the *need* to find security.

"And we find great happiness when we become like a child again, letting our senses guide us as we curiously explore new things."

"Simole, as I think back to my childhood years, I loved being a kid. Even now, I often think about how happy I was, and I've met people who are in their 80s and 90s, and they still think about being a kid after all those years. Is there a reason?"

Simole is smiling. "Ahh… because we will never stop carrying inside of us, the kid we are who is always with us.

"You see Gretchen, the choices we make determine the roads, or as you just witnessed, the trail we take. And in life, each road is waiting with wonderful surprises for us to discover, once we let curiosity and the sense of wonder become our guides once again."

"I think I still have that curiosity, Simole. I mean, geez, look where I am right now. I wouldn't be here unless I followed my curiosity, right?"

Simole nods her head.

"Yes, that's exactly right, my dear."

I stop for a moment and look around.

"Gretchen," she says, "you had said there were two things that impressed you by what you saw on the trail. So tell me, what is the second?"

"Simole, the second is about people in our lives. I'm still puzzled why some people are meant to be with us and others aren't."

"What makes you say that?"

"Look at the animals. Some stay for life, and others just simply want to breed. A lot like many of the guys I've dated."

She bursts out laughing.

"And you know, it really used to bother me, but I guess such is life, isn't it?"

"Gretchen, the people in our lives are like a flowing river, and we are on the bank watching it flow past.

"During our lives, we will meet some who will jump out of the river and stand next to us on the bank to be with us for a long time.

"Others are only out of the river and standing next to us for a short time, before they jump back into the flow of Life's river so they can travel down it in order to be with the next person so they will be the right people in each other's lives for that moment in their lives."

"That's a different way to look at it. Why do you think that is?"

"It's really very simple. Life brings the right people into our lives so that we may teach each other lessons that only we can teach them and only they can teach us. And we come into their lives and they flow down the river of Life into ours, when each is ready at that time in their lives to learn their lessons."

"So why is it that I still get so frustrated at the way some of my friends have changed? It bums me out that it's no longer the same between us as it used to be."

"My dear, does not so much of the misery we feel happen when we keep trying to hold onto the old?

"Or the constant frustration we experience by trying to rekindle something that can't be rekindled and needs to be released? Released and let go to allow whoever it is, to jump back into the flow of the river of Life to their next destination and experience of Life?"

I'm still thinking.

"Every day," she says, "we are changing, all of us; and we will keep changing whether we want to admit it or not. This is Life, and the only thing predictable about it is change.

"Looking at Life, it would appear to these old eyes that the Great Creator loves change, for why would there is so much of it if it wasn't so?

"Life and death. Old and new. For is not every ending a new beginning?"

It's so true.

"Look well to this day, for you, I and everyone else is being changed.

"Cherish, enjoy and learn from those that the river of Life has brought to you.

"But like the fragile butterfly, do not hold those friendships too tightly, for their beauty is best admired from a distance and not too close.

"As you stand on the bank of the river of Life, this time see it and all those who get out and stand on the bank to be with you, from the eyes of an observer, and not one with so many feelings and emotions attached."

"But, that sounds so difficult. How can one really do that?"

"As you experience each person, don't put labels or categorize each friendship or experience as good or bad, happy or sad. Just *let it be what it is and enjoy it and them,* however long you both may have together.

"In our lives, we are not saddened or made joyful by the people and experiences that happen to us, but rather, by our *beliefs* of what happened and how we choose to remember things.

"Choose to look at your experiences differently, and they will be different."

"I'll sure try."

"Gretchen, it's time for you to release all your disappointments and hurts of how you think things *should* be. Things just are.

"My dear, it's time for you to return to *The Path of the Flowing River,* for it is always flowing the right people and experiences into your life at just the right time that you need them.

"Trust it."

Chapter 16

THE SEVENTH TRAIL: "THE PATH OF THE TWO VINES"

*T*his afternoon, as I walk along the seventh trail with Alberto, Simole's nephew, all I can think about is the flowing of the river of Life Simole described, and all the people in my life over the years that have traveled down it.

Still, despite her words of wisdom, at least for now, I can't help experiencing mixed feelings of happiness and some remorse for many of the experiences I've had.

As we hike up the steep road, we descend deep into the jungle.

With machete swinging left to right, Alberto swaths a path in front of us.

I am amazed to see the intricate network of vines, each appearing connected to the others, that appear to go on as far as I can see.

"Alberto, are *all* of these vines connected?"

He stops, wipes his brow and looks around.

"Yes, they are. Each vine strengthens, feeds and protects the others."

"But then what happens to those vines that don't stay connected?"

He points to a brown looking barren vine hanging from a tree.

"You mean like that one?"

"Yes, that one."

"They die, Ms. Gretchen. They die."

We walk another 50 or so yards before we come to a clearing and where we rejoin the original trail.

As we walk, I look all around me, carefully observing which vines are connected and alive and which one's aren't connected and are dead.

Then it hits me.

And no, it isn't a vine.

The vines that are connected are alive because each depends on the other.

Depends on the other for nutrients, water, protection, strength and power so that each can build and continue to grow longer vines to whatever destination Nature has intended.

We finally make it to the clearing to meet Simole.

"Those vines are a lot like people, Simole. A lot like how people need each other."

She looks surprised.

"A vine?"

"Yes! I mean each of those vines needs the others. They need to be connected to grow, to be alive. Aren't we just like them? I mean, don't we need other people in our lives, just like vines need other vines in theirs?"

"And what is it that happens when the vines you describe aren't connected?"

"They die."

"Much like people."

We begin our walk back as Simole begins her talk.

"One of the great mysteries of Life is relationships.

"We are built to be in relationships, to be connected, just like the vines. Yet how strange it seems, that the very thing to bring us so much happiness also brings us so much pain."

"Why do you think that is?"

"Gretchen, as you learned this morning on the trail which led you to understanding *The Path of the Flowing River,* each relationship is meant to be our teacher.

"We learn about ourselves, each other and the world through the experience of being in a relationship.

"Yes, many shy from relationships for fear of being hurt or the relationship's coming to an end, but isn't that the dance of Life—new and old, and every ending a new beginning?"

We stop as she gently cups the bottom of a big beautiful red rose in her hands. "Look at this rose. In the wintertime, it's simply a barren bush and quite unappealing to the eyes. Yet does it not transform itself into something of magnificence, beauty and sweet aroma in only a matter of months?"

I move closer to smell it and nod in agreement.

"The same is true of relationships.

"There will be many times when it doesn't look good to the eyes or feel good to the heart, but if we'll only be patient and give it time, it can bloom.

"You see, Gretchen, to reach the beauty and sweet aroma of the rose, *you must first go over the thorns before you can reach the flower.*"

I like that.

"So why is it, Simole, that I keep going over thorns and never seem to find the flower in my relationships?"

"Let me ask you a question, Gretchen. Is the purpose of a relationship just to have our needs met, perhaps those needs we've carried inside of us since childhood?"

I pause for a moment.

"Probably not."

"And would it not be a mistake to think that another person can fill the emptiness and void that we so easily want them to, and then just as quickly blame them when they don't, when all along, the ability to fulfill that emptiness has and will always be ours?"

"Just what do you mean, Simole?"

"Looking to others for our happiness or to fill the emptiness in our lives is like building the foundation of your relationship house on quicksand.

"The truth is *we* must *first* be happy and complete without a relationship. Then, once we are, once we become the right person for ourselves, we will then be in a much better place in our lives to know when we have found the right person to share our lives with."

"Come on Simole; tell me *how* I can do that."

"We start by accepting the gift that Life has given us by *unconditionally* loving and *accepting* ourselves, right where we are, *regardless* of all the hurts and mistakes we may have made in the past.

"Life asks no more of you than to simply accept the amazing gift It has given you. The gift of being alive!"

She pauses.

"Listen closely, dear Gretchen, *The degree to which you will love and unconditionally accept yourself is the exact degree to which you will do it for others.*

"*That* will *always* be your mirror of where you are at any given point and time in your life."

She stops and looks at me.

"And what, may I ask, is that mirror reflecting back to you today?"

A few moments goes by with not a word spoken. We continue to walk a few yards.

"Stop for a moment, Gretchen. I want us to look at the forest we are in."

We stop.

"Nature is far wiser than we give her credit for.

"Living away in a big city like you do, Gretchen, when you hear word of a fire destroying the rainforest, you feel sad at such a disaster. But such sadness is unnecessary, once you understand the need for Nature's cleansing.

"To look at this jungle, you see vast amounts of vegetation and growth, do you not?"

"It's everywhere you look."

"Yes, my dear. It's as if the forest is wrapped in plants and greenery. But Nature knows far better than us that, left unchecked, many plants in this jungle would grow too wildly, too uncontrollably, and choke off the sunshine and nourishment the other plants and animals need."

"Like the vines."

"Yes, like the vines. And left unchecked, the perfect balance of the jungle would soon disappear, animals and plants would die, and very quickly so too would the life of this jungle.

"Fire, like rain, is one of the ways Nature cleanses the jungle's soul.

"And as quickly as the last ember has burned out, Nature begins at once to replant, re-seed, re-germinate, repopulate and regrow the jungle with all the things the jungle needs, so that it may return to perfect balance.

"So, as it is with the jungle, it must be with our life.

"There must a pruning, a thinning out, and a weeding out of the things in our lives that rob our happiness.

"We must regularly look at those things in our lives and get rid of the beliefs, and anything else, we've allowed that take away our happiness.

"As we get rid of the old beliefs and rid of the weeds, like Nature, we must begin at once to replant and regrow new seeds, the seeds that bring us joy and happiness, and only those things our life now needs.

"The old seeds of the past that bloomed once in our lives are now over, and we feel great freedom and relief the moment we bless and release them. For they helped us reach who and what we've become and helped us get to where we are.

"The moment you plant new seeds is the very moment your life begins with a fresh start."

"Simole, I'm beginning to realize that for too many years of my life, I've been carrying around the hurts, frustrations, anger and disappointments from so many of the experiences I've had, and it's made me miserable, just miserable."

Simole lightly strokes my hair and pats me gently on the back.

"Gretchen, we must forgive anyone and everyone who has ever hurt us, regardless of who they are and what they've done. Forgiveness is a cleansing and healing balm that saturates and soothes our entire being and soul.

"The truth we must know about unforgiveness is this: The only person who stays hurt and will always stay hurt is the unforgiver.

"If you haven't forgotten, then you haven't forgiven."

"But Simole, I've been hurt so many times that it's become so hard for me to forgive like you say."

"I have a question for you, Gretchen. Think back to one of those hurtful times."

She pauses, waiting for me to answer.

"Okay."

"To you, the one experiencing it, it probably felt like something so difficult, so painful, so terrible, didn't it?"

I nod.

"Now, imagine yourself as not the one in the relationship, like you were, but as someone who has never met you before and someone who was simply an outsider observing it all from afar.

"If you were that person, how do you think you would now describe what happened to you?

"And more to the point, do you think you'd be feeling the kind of hurt you have and have continued to carry inside of you all these years?"

I stop and look down for a minute, as I try to imagine myself in someone else's shoes. "I don't think it would bother me."

"That's right.

"You'd probably just say that 'this happened to her and that happened to him and they had a misunderstanding and disagreement and each got upset and each said some hurtful words and they went their separate ways.'

"'Yet all these years, they *keep* holding the feelings of anger and hurt inside of them.'"

"Even after *all* those years…wow."

"Yes, *even* after all those years."

"Don't you see that to someone else, the experiences you had and the things you felt weren't hurtful? *They simply were experiences.*

"*You* were the one who made the decision to attach names to them; hurtful or joyful, happy or sad.

"And *you* have been the one, and the only one, to carry the pain all these years.

"The observer simply witnessed the events in your life without any of the hurtful emotions that have slowly drained your happiness all these years.

"And while you may not be able to change how you felt back then, *you can* change how *you* want to feel *now* and in the future."

I nod my head.

"Simole, do you think it was more because of me or the choices I made back then, that caused so much pain?"

"I think you know, my dear. I think you know."

She's right.

"Many will seek in relationships those who are much like themselves. And as someone who seeks peace and harmony in life, this may be good counsel. Yet we don't truly know the truth about ourselves, our soul and the essence of who we are, and we probably won't—at least in one lifetime. That, my dear, is the joy of the journey and the dance of Life."

She is giving me comfort.

"Each day, each hour, each minute, each second is a clean slate and a new beginning for you to think, feel, experience and relate to yourself and everyone else in a brand new way.

"The choice is yours and will always be. Decide this day, my dear Gretchen, how happy you want to be and give to yourself the gift of forgiveness.

"For if you will forgive a little, a little happiness follows.

"Forgive a lot and much happiness follows.

"Forgive yourself and everyone completely and unconditionally, and peace and joy and harmony and love like you've never known before will be yours.

"Remember what you learned on *The Path of the Two Vines*.

"The gift of Life is for all of us to be connected so that we may have Life and have it with joy and abundance."

Chapter 17

THE EIGHTH TRAIL: "THE PATH OF OUR CALLING"

*A*s the new day dawns on this, the fourth day of my visit, I awaken to new thoughts and feelings.

They are thoughts of feeling differently about myself, and they're unlike those of any day before.

Perhaps with so many new experiences and new understandings coming with them, it is the flood of cleansing of the old to make way for the new.

Whatever it is, I am happy. Really happy.

After a sumptuous breakfast feast, fit for a queen or for somebody learning lessons of Life along the jungle trails, Simole gestures to her sister, Alnea, who will be my guide along the eighth trail.

We bid everyone goodbye, and as we leave Simole tells me, "I'll meet you soon."

Alnea, a simple, yet strikingly beautiful woman, shines with a radiance and a glow that only comes from someone in love.

In love with the rainforest.

As we make our way along the winding path of the trail with a gentle incline, we are surrounded by endless varieties of plants I had not seen on any of the other trails.

I look in amazement, all illuminated from above by the sunlight piercing through the jungle canopy.

"Alnea, these plants are beautiful! So fertile, so lush and so full of colors with such sweet aromas."

"Simole told me she thought you'd love it here. This is my special place where I find such peace and warmth."

We walk deeper into the forest.

I stop. "I never knew so many different kinds of plants and vegetation existed in one place."

Alnea bends down to smell a brightly colored flower with purple, red, yellow and orange hues and gestures for me to come to her. "Gretchen, smell this."

I bend down and inhale. "Oh, does *that* smell good! What is it?"

"It's called the *Bijikaycocus* and it only blossoms for three days all year. Oh, but when it does, it blooms with such beauty and aroma that all the other plants in the jungle must admire it."

I am envious of her passion for the flowers and plants. "Why do you think there are so many different kinds of plants, Alnea?"

"Why do you think there are so many kinds of people?"

I pause. "Perhaps it's because we are all so different?"

"Yes, we are all different; and that's the way it should be, don't you think? It's the desire of Life to express itself in so many different ways."

We walk another 50 yards and then Alnea looks ahead and motions for us to stop.

"Is there something wrong, Alnea?"

"Gretchen, I want you to watch something." She points to the left. "Do you see that big mound of dirt over there?"

"Yes."

"That dirt hill is filled with ants, and they are amazing creatures."

"Ants? Amazing creatures?"

"Oh, yes!"

"How so?"

"Just watch the ant.

"Day in, day out, all day long, the ant goes back and forth along its path carved in the jungle trail, diligently carrying out its tasks that Nature has given it.

"Yet, despite the little ant's tireless efforts, the birds and other animals watching it don't care.

"The birds will watch and squawk and then swoon down to make a mess of the busy ant's hours of hard work and efforts, almost as if to laugh at the tiny moving speck working so hard and so seemingly in vain.

"However, keep watching. The ant simply does not give up. It cannot give up.

"The ant, just like you, is so designed and beautifully created that its success and ability to carry out its task and goal without stopping helps it accomplish its task until that task is finally finished.

"Gretchen, we are just like the ant. We are marvelous creations of the Universe, able to achieve unbelievable things in such a short period of time.

"If only more of us realized it."

Having just witnessed a powerful lesson, I smile as we continue walking.

About ten minutes later, we come to a small stream trickling water along a mossy bank.

There, surrounded by a carpet of one-foot high plants, is a very tall, thin tree that has shot straight up in the air like a skyscraper.

Alnea touches the tree and looks to its top. "Have you ever seen such a tree as this before?"

I study it carefully. "No, I don't think so. What is it?"

"It's called the *Ligjeda,* and it's most amazing."

"Tell me why."

"For the first year of its life, Nature feeds and waters the *Ligjeda* and nothing happens. To see it, you would think it was about ready to die.

"During the second year that Nature feeds and waters it, nothing happens.

"The third year, nothing.

Alnea holds her hands about two feet apart in front of her.

"The fourth and fifth year, still, nothing happens. The *Ligjeda* is just this tall.

"Oh, but on the sixth year that Nature waters and feeds it, in a period of six weeks, the *Ligjeda* awakes from its sleep and grows over 100 feet!"

I look up at its incredible height.

"There's no way! How can that be?"

She smiles.

"When the Great Creator and Nature want to express themselves, they do so in a most majestic way."

As we admire the *Ligjeda*, I am thinking about what she just said about the Great Creator and Nature wanting to express themselves.

For years, I had felt a kind of deep gnawing feeling inside that just didn't want to leave and I didn't know what it was.

Perhaps, like Nature, there was something inside me that wanted to grow and express itself.

Simole meets us at the end of the trail and Alnea smiles at her, as if to say, "We were right. She was amazed."

"So Gretchen, what was your experience this morning?"

"Simole, I never knew I could learn a lesson about anything from simply watching a tiny ant!"

Simole grins. "Ah, the wonderful ant who teaches us that in life, *those who do, are too often ridiculed for their efforts by those who don't.*"

We both laugh.

"Tell me," she asks, "what other experience touched your heart this morning?"

"Simole, never in my life have I seen or heard of the *Ligjeda*. I just can't believe how much it grows so quickly."

She pauses for a moment. "Let me ask you a question: Do you think the *Ligjeda* grew to its magnificent height in six weeks or six years?"

"Six weeks is what Alnea said."

"Yes, she said in six weeks it grew; but what about all the years that Nature watered and fed it?

"Would it have *still* grown if at any time during those six years Nature stopped feeding, watering and taking care of it?"

"I don't know Simole; perhaps not. What are you trying to say?"

"The *Ligjeda* is much like you, Gretchen."

"Me?"

"Yes, Gretchen. Inside of you is the seed, the potential, to grow to magnificent heights.

"There may be many years that you'll work hard, study and practice whatever you love, and little, if anything, will seem to happen.

"But if you keep nourishing your dreams and your hopes, keep feeding and believing them year after year, no matter how hard or long it may take, the day will come, and much sooner than you think, that things will all come together and you, too, will grow as wonderful and magnificent as the *Ligjeda*."

I stop for a moment on the trail.

Simole's words had cut through me to a place that was seeking light, and she had found it.

"Simole, for so many years, I've had this dull ache inside my soul that just won't go away. I've tried to block it out by getting more involved with more projects at work, going out with friends, moving to a new city and being in different relationships; but despite what I do, it *always* follows me."

"Dear child, what you're feeling is the Great Creator calling out to you to express the incredible abilities you, and only you, have; to help others and bring yourself joy."

"But, I've been afraid."

She laughs. "Oh, goodness. Haven't we all, my dear? Haven't we all?

"But I want you think about this. If we are surrounded by the goodness and love of Nature and the Great Creator that gave you the gift of Life and created you for a special purpose, would it not be some mean and cruel joke if that same Creator gave you such a powerful desire to express it, without also giving you all the ability you will ever need to achieve it?"

I ask if we can sit down.

We find a hollowed log as she begins.

"The desire inside you is the desire that's calling for you to let it out; and by using it to bless others, to let it show you what true happiness is all about. Happiness you have never known.

"Look at the misery you've felt by accepting less than your heart has told you that you are capable of."

Simole sees my sadness.

She places her gentle hand under my chin as she lifts my head up and looks into my eyes.

"What you *are,* my dear Gretchen, is a gift from the Great Creator.

"What you *become* is *your* gift to you and to all those around you and to those you may never know.

"My precious one, when you are doing the things you love and expressing your gifts, talents and abilities that the Great Creator has given you, through the desires you feel deep inside, then Life becomes so easy, so joyful, so fulfilling, so worth every breath you take.

"And it will always be so, when you follow your heart and its desires as they lead you down *The Path of Our Calling.*"

Chapter 18

THE NINTH TRAIL: "THE PATH OF THE ABUNDANT"

*L*ike a great curtain that is being pulled back to reveal a new scene, the jungle sky quickly goes from light to dark as I trek along the ninth trail with Ernesto, Simole's brother. Afternoon rains pour ribbons of water on our heads.

Already, I like this trail, for it's filled with banana and orange trees, luscious red and succulent berry plants, and other fruits I've never seen in the produce section of any supermarket.

This time, having gotten the hang of following this trail stuff by now, I pass Ernesto on the trail.

I stop to fill my mouth with a few strawberries.

Ernesto smiles as I hand him a big juicy berry I picked, and I start talking with my mouth half full.

"Ernesto, you must be in heaven with all this delicious fruit just outside your back door."

He takes a bite from the strawberry. "It is delicious, Señorita. We've enjoyed the fruit on this mountain ever since I was a child."

"Really. How long has your family lived here?"

"Oh, goodness, as far back as any of us can remember. The jungle and the Mountain have always been our home."

As we start to walk again, Ernesto describes the plants we're seeing and the different kinds of animals that depend on them for survival.

"The *Pylia* bird needs the *Ugeru* plant to give it the nutrients it cannot get from anywhere else. And the *Sigiando* tree gives nectar to the bees, which pollinate the *Ugeru* plant."

"They are all so connected, Ernesto; they all need each other. So what happens if the birds don't have any *Ugeru* plants to eat or the *Sigiando* tree doesn't give nectar?"

"Oh they never have to worry about that, Ms. Gretchen, because Nature *always* provides abundance for all its creatures."

Looking all around at the plethora of animals, birds, plants, flowers and trees, it's easy to see the incredible harvest of abundance that covers the forest floor and fills the jungle sky. Every animal and plant is provided for by Nature, and not a better provider could they find.

Watching the *Pylia* bird eat from the *Ugeru,* as the bees travel from tree to plant and back again, seemingly without a care in the world, leaves me impressed that if the Great Creator cares in such intricate detail about them, how much would It care for and provide for me?

This time, Simole doesn't wait to greet us at the end of the trail; she meets us halfway from the other side.

As we are still watching the dance of Life ritual between bird and plant, tree and bee, Simole speaks softly. "Wonderful, isn't it, how Nature provides for all its creatures?"

"Oh, yeah. I mean look at what's going on right now with just this bird and that plant, those bees and that tree. And the amazing thing is the countless other similar things going on in the jungle right now that we can't see. There are just so many choices."

As we get up and work our way back to the end of the trail, Simole begins the lesson.

"The Great Creator gives abundance to all the creatures, large or small, on this earth.

"In our life, we always have an abundance of choices.

"So many choices that we often don't realize just how many we have, do you agree?"

"I totally agree, Simole."

"Gretchen, we limit ourselves by holding on to the limiting and life-draining beliefs we continue to carry of how we should live of lives according to what others think, and not by following our deepest heart's desire and the calling of the Universe, which always knows the best path our lives should take.

"For even in the jungle, one can see how Nature gives the power of choice to even the animals. Look at the monkeys."

We stop for a moment and admire them from a distance.

"Of all the fruit they can eat, *they always seek out the best and let go of the rest,* for the best fruit, the ripest fruit, is also the most delicious and fulfilling.

"No one tells the monkey which ones to pick.

"Instinctively, they just *know.*"

"But *how* do they know, Simole?"

"They know because they *listen* to the voice inside of them.

"It's the *same* voice that you have inside of you.

"When we listen to the voice inside our hearts—that same instinct from the very source all the animals receive it from—and follow its call, we begin to *let go of the things that no longer work in our lives, so that our hands and hearts can now hold on to those that will.*

"You see, my dear, you have the power to accept only the things in life that are good for you, the best things for your life's journey and, yes, those that you want.

"And all you need to do is simply *find what's best and then let go of the rest.*"

Simole catches me in deep thought and smiles. "A peso for your thoughts, my dear?"

I smile with bewilderment. "Simole, I still am amazed that each thing in the jungle depends on Nature to provide for it to survive. What if it doesn't? I mean, that can be a scary thought."

"Did the animals and birds look nervous to you that they wouldn't be provided for?"

"No. They probably don't even know or care. It's just probably some biological urge that it's time to seek food and they go get it."

"Ah... but *what* is it that gives them that urge to seek food and *what* is it that guides them to the right food they need for their specific needs?"

"Nature, right?"

"Yes. And if Nature has put the urge to seek the kinds of food they need in their little heads, doesn't it also provide that food in abundance and show them where they may find it?"

"Yes. Nature *is* amazing and so abundant."

"And, even though the animals in the jungle may not know what it is or perhaps consciously use it, could we not say that the animals and all living things have a kind of unspoken trust that depends on Nature and the Great Creator to provide the abundance in their lives so that they can live, survive and perpetuate?"

"I think so."

"So Gretchen, how has Nature and the Great Creator showed Their abundance in your life?"

"Well, like the animals, I, too, think I have a kind of trust that I use. But, more times than not, I pretty much feel that whatever happens in my life is a result of *my* actions, so I've got to depend on myself or else it won't happen."

"And what about the things that you *don't* want to happen?" Are these also the result of *your* actions?"

I ponder for a few seconds. "They probably are, but many times I wonder how that can be, since I'm always working so hard to make good things happen. I mean, when I think of all the bad stuff that seems to come my way, even though I'm trying so hard to do the right things, I sometimes feel like Life is unfair."

"Gretchen, as you've just seen, Life is abundant and provides for all Its creatures, does it not?"

"Yes."

"And while the animals depend on Life to feed and provide for them, the animals don't have what we have: the ability to use our thoughts and to direct them *any* way *we* want.

"Our trust and belief in ourselves activates and sets Life in motion to help us. The trust and belief we have in ourselves gives Life the power to move in our lives in mysterious ways.

"But we must believe in It, trust It and use It, if we are ever to get the results we want."

"So how can I do that when it seems so difficult?"

"Simply ask Life to show you Its power. Ask Life to show you that It hears your calling and belief. Then get out of the way and let It show you Its amazing power of what It can do in your life right now."

"But Simole, you don't understand. I've tried that, and nothing seems to happen; or if it does, things seem to turn out wrong. That's not the kind of belief I want."

"But it's the kind of belief you're using. You've just turned Its power *against* you instead of *helping* you."

I'm getting fumed.

"That's crazy! Why on earth would I want to do something as foolish as that?"

"Because Life listens to your *words* and *belief* and It will bring you whatever you deeply believe. So, if you've been having bad things, as you say, come your way, what does that tell you?"

I pause and look around.

"I don't know; that... that I've been bringing these problems on *myself*? How do I do that?"

"If things keep bringing us unhappiness and pain in our lives, have we not used the power of our thoughts and belief, but in a way that brings us an abundance of troubles?"

I nod.

"And has not Life heard our call and answered by giving us what our thoughts and belief asked for?"

"It sounds to me as if you're saying that *I* am asking to be hurt and miserable. Simole, that's absurd."

"You, dear Gretchen, have been thinking of the things you *don't* want to happen. But thinking of what you don't have or what you want to change in your life, only creates *more* of those things which you *don't want.*"

"Say that again, Simole."

"If your thoughts and beliefs are more focused on how to avoid the things that are bringing you pain and unhappiness, *instead* of filling your mind with thoughts of things that you *do* want to happen, then Life, being neutral and playing no favorites with anyone, will answer whatever thinking and belief you give it, with the attitudes, expectations and experiences that perfectly match your thoughts and belief."

I see where she's going with this.

"Okay, let me see if I've got this right. So what you're saying is, *I need to keep my mind on the things I want and off of the things I don't want?*"

"That's *exactly* what I'm saying, Gretchen."

"Our lives will be filled with all the abundance we could ever imagine—far more than what your eyes will ever see in this rainforest—if we have the right thoughts, the right beliefs, and take the right inspired actions that will allow Life and the Great Creator to bring them to us.

"We must always remember that just as our thinking, our ability to dream and imagine and believe, is unlimited, so too is Life and Its ability to provide for those dreams and belief.

"Our lives can change as little or as much as we want, if we'll just have enough trust and belief in ourselves and allow the Great Creator to guide our steps along *The Path of the Abundant.*"

Chapter 19

THE TENTH TRAIL: "THE PATH TO THE WISE"

*M*y journey on the Mountain is almost over, and I have learned so much along the nine trails during the four days I have traveled them.

Never in my wildest dreams could I have imagined that so many lessons about life could be learned from Nature, in the most unlikely of places, and from the most unlikely of people.

It all seems so much like a fantasy; if it all ended right here, right now, it wouldn't matter.

My life has changed and I've found a wisdom and happiness I know will be with me until the end of my days.

But it isn't about to end.

There is still one last trail to follow.

The Tenth Trail.

The most important of all trails, Simole told me; and for this one, only she will be my guide.

The words she spoke of—"You're about to meet the wisest person you will ever know"—each day we met, and the many talks we had, have kept ringing in my head ever since I heard her speak them.

I now know, coming from her and considering all the other words of wisdom she spoke, it is a statement of most significant meaning.

This morning we meet at the appointed time on the crossroads where all trails converged except one.

The Tenth Trail.

Simole approaches. "Are you ready to begin your journey?"

"Yes, I think so."

Simole tucks her hand around the inside of my arm and pulls me close to her side as we begin walking.

"My Gretchen, never be afraid of who you will meet and what you will find here on the Mountain or anywhere you may travel. For is not the beauty of Life, all the uncertainty and surprises it contains?"

I nod my head and smile as we continue our walk along The Tenth Trail.

Of all the trails I have traveled, this one is the most different.

Never have I seen such beautiful flowers and varieties of plants and so many different animals.

It is as if Nature seems to bow in respect to this amazing woman, among the wisest of humans who've walked the planet.

For never until now have I witnessed her "Dr. Doolittle" effect on the animals, as they watch and chatter with each step we make, winding up the trail.

"What do you see, Gretchen?"

"I see animals that look so calm, so happy. I've never seen anything like this before."

"Do you understand why this may be as you say?"

"Because they know you and know you won't harm them?"

"Ah… you're on the right path. But could it also be because we are in Nature's perfect timing with every movement and every breath, and our thoughts are unhurried, calm and peaceful and in the *flow* of Life?"

"Yes Simole, I think so."

"The animals understand and respond to not only to the sound of our voices, but to our actions and movement. If we are at peace with ourselves, we are at peace with Nature, and Nature responds in kind."

We slowly continue our walk.

"In all of Nature, silence is powerful. We cannot hear a tree grow, yet we know it does.

"We cannot hear baby birds grow bigger wings for flight, but we know they do.

"And we cannot hear our thoughts and lives changing with every moment of every day of our lives, yet we know they have and always will.

"If we are to be guided by the Great Creator, we must listen to our inner voice that speaks to us best when we are silent and at peace with all those around us, especially ourselves.

"We must get in Life's perfect timing for our lives and be calm and centered as we follow our heart's desires, but not forcing things to happen before Life is *ready* for them to happen."

My steps slow down, and then I pause for a moment as I turn to her.

"Simole?"

"Yes?"

"This wisest of all persons whom I'm about to meet…"

"Yes?"

"How do you know I will think they are as wise as you say?"

She smiles. "A wonderful question, my dear. I see you've learned your lessons on the Mountain well."

I smile.

Nearly a minute passes as we continue walking while I wait for her answer. Suddenly she stops and looks at me.

"Because many years ago, this was the wisest person I ever met. It was the wisest person your friend Chloe ever knew, and it's been the wisest person anyone who has journeyed along this same road has ever known… and it will be the same for you, too."

My heart begins beating faster with anticipation.

As we ascend high along the trail to the top of the Mountain, Simole stops, and I look over at her in surprise.

"Is there something wrong, Simole?"

Simole reaches into her pocket and pulls out a black bandanna and with one end in each hand, moves toward my face.

"*Now* is the time you must put this on."

She gently wraps the dark cloth around my head, completely covering my eyes.

I stand motionless and silent.

She grabs my arm and tucks it back close to her body and we begin walking slowly.

As we walk, my nose smells sweet and different aromas.

As we continue walking higher up the Mountain, my ears hear birds singing melodies and tones different from any I've heard on the Mountain.

Wait.

What's that?

It sounds like water splashing. A waterfall?

Yes, it must be a waterfall. Where?

"Simole, where are we?"

"Shhh, my dear. We are almost there."

We walk another minute. We stop.

She reaches behind my head and gently unties the knot. The bandanna slips down.

My eyes open wide in awe. This is paradise.

Wild orchids, daffodils, roses of purple, yellow, red, white and every color, tulips, daisies, petunias, flowered vines, bushes and majestic trees everywhere.

Swans, geese, ducks, monkeys, squirrels, rabbits and all the different kinds of exotic birds I had seen on the Mountain.

As my head keeps turning from side to side, up and down and every which way, I'm breathless, standing frozen in my shoes.

"Oh, Simole… *never* have I seen a place filled with *such* beauty!"

She looks at me and smiles. She holds out both arms to the incredible sights before my eyes. *"This* is *my* gift to you.

"Are you ready to meet who we've come to meet?"

I slowly snap out of my trance. "Oh yes, Simole. I know this is the moment I've waited for."

"Longer than you may have realized."

We walk a few more steps as she leads me through the garden. As we walk to the edge, Simole stops.

"Gretchen, close your eyes once more and cover them with your hands.

"We must walk only a short way farther and we will be there."

A few steps later, we stop. The sounds and the air have stilled.

"Kneel down, Gretchen. We are here."

I bend down in great reverence and respect, knowing that I'm about to meet the wisest of all persons.

Simole whispers.

"Slowly… now… open your eyes."

I do.

"What do you see?"

I look in front of me. "I see a pool of crystal clear water… it's like glass."

"Yes, but is that *all* you see?"

On my knees, with hands resting against the tops of my legs, I look around.

Simole whispers. "Gretchen, when your face looks down, tell me… what does it see?"

I look.

I stare.

I look again.

I pause.

Tears begin streaming down my cheeks.

"I… I see *me*."

Simole sniffs, as she tries to hold back her tears.

"And *who* is it that you see looking back at *you*?"

I look down again.

"It is *me*, Simole… it is *me*."

For moments, not a word is spoken.

My body starts shaking as the words slide from my lips. "I, Simole; *I am*... that wise person you said I would meet?"

"Yes, Gretchen. *It is you.*"

My eyes can't stop looking at the reflection.

Never had I *seen* myself before.

Simole bends down and begins stroking my hair and holding it in her loving hands.

Tears begin to gush from my eyes as I turn to her.

"My dear Gretchen, all your life you've been so hard on yourself."

"You've suffered so much pain that you were never meant to. You've kept joys from your heart that Life meant for you to have. You, dear Gretchen, are so precious to the Great Creator, and all those around you."

I wrap my arms around her and hug her with all the love in my heart.

In my ear she whispers, "Oh, Dear One, be filled with joy and love. For you, my child, my dear Gretchen, have just met the wisest person you will ever know... and... the best friend you will ever have."

Chapter 20

THE LAST DAY ON THE MOUNTAIN

The day has arrived that I will leave the Mountain. Inside, I am feeling both happy and sad.

Sad, that I will leave Simole, her family and this beautiful place; yet happy to return home to begin my life anew with an understanding I never imagined possible only days ago.

As I enjoy one last breakfast with Simole and her family, I look at her and ask a question.

"Simole, words cannot even begin to express my gratitude for how you and your family have changed my life. I would like to repay you for your kindness, so please, tell me, what you would like and I will be happy to give it to you."

Simole smiles, as she looks all around the table to each family member who is also smiling.

"Gretchen, all the money in the world could never buy what you and all of us have experienced together."

I look around at everyone and smile.

"But there is one thing that I ask that you do," she says.

"Of course, Simole. Anything."

"Just like Maxwell and your friend Chloe did for you, I want you to share your experience with those who are *ready* to hear the message, for the Great Creator will bring whoever they may be to you and you to them at just the perfect time in both of your lives. Would you do this for me?"

"Simole, to do so will be one of the greatest joys of my life."

We finish our breakfast and make our way down the Mountain.

As we reach the bottom, there waiting for us with a big grin on his face and with my horse is Fernando, my guide back to town.

I greet Fernando.

Off in the distance I hear horses approaching from the trail.

As the horses make their way into the clearing, I see an older man on one horse and a younger man on the other.

The horses come closer and stop near Fernando and me.

Fernando greets his older friend on horseback as the young man on the other horse looks around in amazement.

I know why he's here.

After Fernando finishes his conversation, I ask him to wait for just a few moments.

I walk over to the young man on his horse, grab his hand and help him get down.

"Welcome. What is your name?"

"My name is Austin."

"Well, Austin, it is good to have you here on the Mountain."

I point to the hollowed out tree where I first sat days ago as I hand him a cup of cool water.

"Come and sit down for a moment. "May I tell you a story?"

"Of course."

My story begins…

Chapter 21

THE LAST DAY IN TOWN

*A*s the taxi slowly pulls up and stops in front of Javiar's shop, I look at all the people and shops that line the street and remember my first night here.

Oh, what an experience this has been.

This is the day I am leaving to return home, and I promised Javiar I would see him before I leave.

The taxi driver unloads my suitcases in front of Javiar's shop and, with pesos in hand, speeds off.

Javiar sees me and with a big enthusiastic smile waves me to come inside.

He plays coy.

"Señorita, you've come back. Tell me about your trip."

"Javiar, I don't even know where to begin."

I know he's heard the answer many times before, but still he asks.

"Was it all you imagined it would be?"

"Never in my life, Javiar, have I had such a life-changing experience, nor have I met anyone as wise as Simole."

"Yes, Señorita, Simole is the wisest person our people know. She is known all over the world by people, just like you, who are changed in ways they could never imagine. This, Señorita, is the legend of Simole and the Mountain."

"I know now that before I left for the Mountain you couldn't tell me about her or what I would experience on the journey."

"How is it that I, Javiar, an old carver, could tell *you* anything that *you* would not find out for *yourself*?"

"Well Javiar, for an old carver, you didn't get the wisdom that goes along with that gray hair for nothing."

We both laugh.

"Señorita, before you go, I have something for you."

He bends down and reaches under his table.

He holds out his hands to give me a wrapped box.

"Here, *this* is my gift to you. Take this home and remember our people and the time you spent in Partangia."

I am taken with surprise.

"Javiar, *I* should be the one giving *you* the gift."

He looks at me and smiles. "To have met someone as beautiful and lovely as you, that is the only gift these old eyes need."

"I can't even begin to thank you for what you've done for me."

"Yes, Señorita, I think you can. Promise me that you will not open the box until you are on the plane and flying home. Will you do this for me?"

"Of course, Javiar. Of course."

"Good." The look on Javiar's face turns serious. "I have arranged for Fernando to take you to the airport in his truck." Fernando comes out from the back room smiling.

"His *truck?*"

Javiar and Fernando burst out laughing.

"Well, unfortunately for you, Fernando needs his truck, so he called a taxi. I hope this will be okay."

I chuckle. "I'll try not to be too disappointed."

Five minutes later, a small yellow taxi pulls in front of the shop and honks its horn.

Before I leave, Javiar looks at me with a schoolboy shyness. "May I shake your hand goodbye?"

As I reach my arms around him, I say, "No, I'm giving you a big hug. Thank you, Javiar. I will always remember you in my heart."

"Me too, Gretchen. Me too."

Gretchen.

I'm not Señorita anymore.

Chapter 22

THE PLANE RIDE I'LL NEVER FORGET

*A*s the last of my bags have just been checked, with ticket in hand I walk out on the tarmac to my plane.

I'm happy.

No… make that *really* happy.

As I'm walking towards the noisy turbo-prop puddle jumper called my plane, this time I couldn't care less if it's a cramped tuna can that'll bounce around like a kite in the air. It's going to feel like sitting first class in a 747 to me.

I take my seat and stuff my bag under the seat in front of me.

A few minutes go by. The cabin door is closed and the engines start and begin to whirl.

The plane's wheels move and we start to taxi.

The plane's engines whine as we gather speed.

Suddenly, the nose lifts up off the ground.

As I look out the window, all I can see is dense forest and jungle, as if Partangia never existed.

If only the people sitting with me knew what kind of life-changing experience could be waiting for them there, hidden in all the trees just below.

I reach down to grab my purse, and as I rifle through it looking for some mints or gum, I feel the box Javiar has given to me.

It is time to open it.

I push the button overhead to turn on the little reading light.

I slowly peel away the newspaper wrapping that's bound by string and tape. I want to save the paper, string and even the tape as a souvenir.

As the paper lies flat on my lap, I open the box.

Inside is a fairly heavy object.

It feels like something hard; like a stone.

I slowly unwrap the tissue paper covering it and with the last piece of tissue peeled away, there it is: a piece of exquisitely cut stone in the shape of a small mountain.

Wow, that was so nice of Javiar.

I admire it a few seconds more before getting ready to wrap it back up.

As I pick it up, I turn it over and see something surprising.

There are letters carved on the bottom.

How strange.

I have never seen anything like this before.

I pick it up and examine the letters closer.

Why... it's my name.

Wait. It's not just my name; it's my signature, exactly inscribed the way I sign it!

Then it hits me.

So that's why Javiar asked me to sign my name on a piece of paper before I left for the Mountain.

But there is something more. Something at the bottom of the box. It's a note from Javiar.

I open it. It reads:

To my friend Gretchen,

Here is the only part of you that wasn't changed.

Your friend,

Javiar

I'm speechless. Chills travel through me as tears begin to flow.

As I lean back and look out the window, the happiest smile inside me bubbles to the surface.

I know Javiar is right.

My life and my world changed because of him, Simole and her people.

It changed because I went to the Mountain and what they taught me and I learned along the Ten Trails of Wisdom.

No longer will I see my life and those in it through the same eyes.

Then I realize something, so simple, yet so powerful.

My life has changed because *I* have changed.

And it all began on the day I decided to *Go Tell It on the Mountain.*

The End

...Or Is It the Beginning?

Be the first to get the next release of
GO TELL IT ON THE MOUNTAIN

Go to www.RobertWolff.com and click on the
New Books Coming Soon tab
For all the details.
Thank You and Best Wishes!